PRACTICAL ORGANIC GARDENING

PRACTICAL
ORGANIC GARDENING

by

BEN EASEY

revised and edited by

BRIAN FURNER

FABER AND FABER LTD

3 Queen Square

London

First published in 1955
New and revised edition 1976
Faber and Faber Limited
3 Queen Square London WC1
Printed in Great Britain by
Whitstable Litho Ltd Whitstable Kent
All rights reserved

ISBN 0 571 10314 6

CONTENTS

ILLUSTRATIONS

Diagrams

ABOUT THIS BOOK

Organic gardening is a system of maintaining and increasing the fertility of the garden soil by applying waste products to it. These wastes such as crop remains, animal manures and garbage are usually fermented in compost heaps before being applied to the soil. Gardeners who garden by organic methods are convinced that they are working in harmony with natural laws. The organic system of soil fertilization leads to no soil pollution, does not lead to dangerous chemical reactions in the soil and prevents erosion of soil by wind and rain. Those who practise organic methods observe the general good health of their garden plants and obtain from them crops which are the envy of the less fortunate and less knowledgeable. The practice of organic methods is not in itself a short cut to successful gardening. The gardener must have a good understanding of the requirements of his or her garden plants and a knowledge of the many differing cultural techniques for optimum results. These practical aspects of gardening are covered well in books dealing with the cultivation of food crops. In this book the author assumes that the reader is not ignorant of practical garden work but is anxious to apply organic methods.

Above all the author guides the reader to have that special approach towards the soil and to the environment—an approach which separates the organic gardener from most others. The organic gardener sees the soil as something precious, practises conservation and fights pollution. Those who garden organically oppose the nineteenth-century chemical approach to plant feeding. The chemical school of thought appeared to ignore the physical and biological qualities of soil and to treat it as inert matter of use primarily as an anchorage for plant roots. Instead of maintaining and increasing soil fertility it was considered that factory-made chemicals could be applied to the soil and these applications would suffice for good cropping. The chemicals contained the major plant foods—nitrogen,

11

phosphorus and potassium (*kalium*). Many gardeners still use these chemicals which the organic enthusiast considers as harmful soil pollutants.

Ben Easey wrote this work between 1952 and 1955, I myself became a keen organic gardener in 1950, but it was not until after I had read his book that I met the author whose sad death at a young age meant a loss of a very active supporter of the organic movement in Great Britain. What Ben Easey wrote more than twenty years ago did not appear relevant then. Conservation, pollution, organically-raised food crops, erosion were not subjects of great debate in the fifties. Now, not only are these subjects discussed on radio and television and in the national press, they are also discussed generally in our schools and in our homes. Ben Easey wanted us all not only to discuss; he wanted us also to take practical steps starting off in our own gardens to practise conservation, to fight pollution, to prevent erosion and to grow health-giving wholefood for our families.

I hope that the publication of a slightly updated, abbreviated edition of his book will guide many more gardeners to put Ben Easey's suggestions to a practical test in their own gardens. Such a test costs you nothing. I can only hope that your results will please you. Tasting and eating organically grown food harvested from your own garden is really something. Not only do the fruit and vegetables taste good—they are good.

BRIAN FURNER

CHAPTER I

WHY ORGANIC GARDENING?

The forest, jungle or prairie, populated by vegetation and organisms ranging from bacteria to buffaloes, maintains a stable balance of fertility. Living is on 'income', as it were, one form of life or the by-products of it becomes the food of another. In some cases 'savings' are actually built up. These may be in the form of peat, a miser's hoard locked up for centuries by acidity and climate, or in the form of coal. A universal storehouse is the rich, deep loam of virgin land, which is capable of supporting many successive crops even after its income of organic matter has been cut off. But it can be swiftly rifled and its reserves spent and overdrawn by those who farm or garden without thought for the future, and the cost becomes apparent when the soil produces its 'pass book' at the end of several seasons or a decade and a 'debit' balance shows in the red figures of uneconomic yield, erosion and, finally, dustbowls and deserts.

Out of the closed cycle of fertility maintenance operated by nature, man must take practically all his food, largely his clothing and many other of the commodities he uses, and he cannot be content with these on nature's scale. Of the inflated populations made possible by more sure means of survival (including the health service), some members are plainly parasitic on food production because they do not contribute to it, directly or indirectly. Man, as farmer or gardener, therefore contrives to increase production by methods which are now common: by growing selected plants in individual fields, whereas in nature they are spread over large areas as 'weeds'; by selecting, cultivating and improving crop varieties to provide more of the roots, foliage, fruit and flowers for which they are grown; and also by manuring his land.

WHY ORGANIC GARDENING?

If we could manage with these crops on the production scale of the Broadbalk field at Rothamsted Experimental Station, which has been cropped since 1844 without the addition of fertilizers of any kind, and still yields 6½ cwt. of wheat per acre instead of rather more than the ton an average farmer harvests, there would probably be no need of manures of any kind, whether natural or 'artificial'. The top 9 inches of a fertile acre of soil in a temperate climate contains roughly enough essential plant foods for over a hundred crops. But only a fraction of each food is in a form in which plants can absorb it, for these have evolved to take their nourishment from minerals and decaying organic matter mainly in the forms in which it is made available by 50,000 lb. of fungi and bacteria in the fertile top layer of an acre of soil.

Without a supply of nitrogen in usable form, no plant is able to take up any other nutriment from the soil, or even from a hydroponic solution. Out of the four-fifths of this element in the air, 4 to 7 lb. per acre per year is 'fixed' by thunderstorms and rain falling all over the land and sea surface of the world, and a tiny fraction, mainly as calcium cyanamide and nitro-chalk, is produced by man's use of electric power. Far greater quantities than these are made by the unseen soil population. It has been estimated that 25 lb. of nitrogen per year may be fixed in the top layer of an acre of fertile soil by two types of free-living ('non-symbiotic') bacteria, *Clostridia* and *Azotobacter*. For this mysterious process of fixation, these organisms require air, minerals and energy food in the form of the starches and sugars (carbohydrates) of decaying organic matter—needs which, incidentally, the organic gardener abundantly satisfies. The energy for the process of fixation operated by yet another organism, *Bacillus radicicola*, comes from the plant with which it co-operates. This bacterium lives and multiplies in galls or nodules, which it forms on the roots of leguminous plants. In return for carbohydrates extracted from their host, enormous numbers of the root-nodule bacteria contribute nitrogen, which they import in an insoluble form from the air and convert in their bodies. Some of these 'conjurors' are absorbed by the plant during its growth, others die when their carbohydrate supply diminishes at the end of their host plant's growing season and, with their nitrogen cargo, are carried into the soil in the nodule which sloughs off the plant's roots. It has been estimated that, under favourable conditions, co-operation between this organism and Wild White Clover has resulted in the fixation of over 400 lb. of

14

nitrogen per acre in a single year, and the equivalent of 40 cwt. of sulphate of ammonia during a two-year partnership with American Sweet Clover (*Melilotus alba*). Further increase to the supplies of nitrogen in the soil is made by mycorrhiza (fungi), which co-operate with 80 per cent at least of our flowering plants, including all common crops except tomatoes, potatoes and some brassicas. Under suitable conditions, as in nature or on a fertile organic garden, plant roots are invaded by the mycelium of the mycorrhizal fungus, which then lives partly inside the roots and partly outside in the soil. In return for carbohydrate energy foods, the fungus contributes moisture, nitrogen and other nutrients to the plant which finally absorbs the mycellium into its own tissues. 'Mycorrhizal association', as this symbiotic relationship between plant and fungus is called, occurs only to a limited degree, or not at all, in soils containing much free nitrogen. Highly nitrogenous manures, whether organic or inorganic, by indirectly raising the nitrogen content of plants reduce or prevent fixation by mycorrhiza, as well as by the root-nodule bacteria of the leguminosae. They may also discourage earthworms, of which there may be eight million to the acre of fertile land and whose casts may amount in a single year to a deposit of many tons. These have been found normally to contain five times as much nitrogen, three times as much available magnesium, seven times as much available phosphate and eleven times as much available potash as the surrounding soil.

Of course, not all is on the credit side of the nitrogen balance sheet. Whilst some bacteria and fungi 'fix' nitrogen from the air or release it from the protein constituents of decaying organic matter, and convert it into forms suitable for absorption by plants, other organisms do the very reverse and throw back some of the gains into the air. The amount lost by this process of 'denitrification' in soils cannot accurately be assessed. Where a great loss of nitrogen can occur is in the mishandling of farmyard manure which contains vastly more nitrogen than is removed in meat and wool sold off the land. Of the nitrogen contained in animal foodstuffs, 6·2 per cent is recovered in meat, but more than 80 per cent goes into the dung and urine of animals and, of this between 20 and 40 per cent may be lost during normal methods of manure production. The 'denitrifying' organisms are, of course, used by man in the modern septic tank system of sewage treatment, but they are kept at a minimum in the well-aerated compost heap in which the nitrogen-fixing bacteria are favoured. In cultivated soils lacking in organic matter there is also often serious loss of nitrogen because this element is leached in drainage water after heavy rains.

Under natural conditions, by means of nitrogen-fixation and conversion of this element from one form to another and back again, organisms maintain in the soil a balance of roughly one part of nitrogen in available form to ten parts of carbon-containing compounds in a state of decay. If the gardener cultivates into his soil raw organic matter, comparatively low in nitrogen (such as straw, of which the carbon/nitrogen ratio is about 30/1), the carbon concentration is raised in relation to the available nitrogen. As there is insufficient of this available nitrogen in the straw to provide energy for the enormous numbers of microbes which attack and break it down, the extra supplies of this element needed are taken from the soil. It is only slowly released back into the soil as and when the excess carbon in the sugars, starches and celluloses is dispersed, the organic matter is broken down and the organisms which have done the job themselves die and decay because food supplies are diminished or exhausted. This results in a period of temporary 'nitrogen starvation'. The lack of the amount of available nitrogen which is borrowed from the soil and taken into fungal and bacterial protoplasm during the dispersal of the extra twenty parts of carbon in straw, can mean stunted seedlings and retarded plant growth for several weeks. With sawdust, which has a carbon/nitrogen ratio near 250/1, robbery is much more serious and may last for several months or even years.

If, on the other hand, the gardener cultivates into his soil a highly nitrogenous manure, whether organic or inorganic, he prevents or reduces fixation of nitrogen by bacteria and fungi and, in addition, may cause a reduction in the humus-content of the soil. Young, fresh green manure is highly nitrogenous and contains but little humus-forming material. If it is cultivated under the soil surface it raises a dense crop of those organisms which attack, feed on it, decompose it, then, stimulated by the excess nitrogen still remaining, proceed to 'burn up' also some of the more resistant organic matter (humus) in the soil. This is detrimental to the soil.

A green crop of near-mature lupins has a supply of nitrogen in the nodules on its roots and may be incorporated into the soil without fear of causing temporary 'nitrogen starvation'. When a mature, non-leguminous green manure is turned under, additional nitrogen in the form of animal dung may be dug in, too. Although in neither case

16

may nitrogen-robbery or humus-loss be caused, nevertheless, the soil will for some considerable time contain a great mass of undigested organic matter and be unsuitable for habitation by plants. In addition, the quantity of nitrogen in 3 tons of poultry manure to the acre may be needed to remove the robbery danger from a good stand of high-cellulose mature mustard.

If the gardener is to exploit to the full the sources of 'free' nitrogen and is also to reduce to a minimum the losses of this essential plant food by 'denitrification' or its 'locking up' by soil organisms, he must regulate carefully his treatment of the soil, especially so far as its manuring is concerned. He needs to use his nitrogenous manures (always scarce) as economically as possible and without causing depletion of the soil's stock of humus and, particularly if he is running a commercial, intensively-cropped garden, he cannot delay sowing or planting until nitrogen, temporarily locked up by the addition to the soil of undecomposed organic matter, is again released and planting conditions are once more suitable. To keep up the supply of nitrogen and to maintain and increase the humus-content of his soil, the organic gardener provides abundant organic matter, mature or near-mature, raw or part-decayed, on or near the soil surface, especially in the autumn when nitrogen, a readily-leached element is most liable to be washed from the soil. The nitrogen which fungi and bacteria absorb from the protein constituents of such slowly-decayed organic matter or compost is anchored in their bodies during the period when heaviest rains occur in a temperate climate. It is then slowly released into the soil—when bacteria and fungi die and decay because food supplies are diminished and droughts and rains occur—in the quantity and steady supply required to see plants right through the growing season to harvesting. Further nitrogen is made available by the free-living nitrogen-fixing organisms which are encouraged by a surface mulch of decaying organic matter and leaching is prevented or reduced, both of nitrogen and of other minerals.

The top 9 inches of an acre of fertile soil contains, on average, 2,750 lb. of phosphorus and 6,750 lb. of potash, and the lower layers even more of these minerals, and others, mainly in an insoluble form. Some quantities of phosphates (apart from the small amounts deposited in falling rain), potash and other minerals are dissolved out of the soil and kept 'available' by the weak acid solution of carbon dioxide produced during the breakdown of organic matter by fungi, bacteria and the digestive processes of earthworms. Some plants can extract from the soil at least part of their own requirements of some minerals, by excreting an organic acid from their roots. A crop of American Sweet Clover has been found to raise the soil content of both available phosphate and potash from the analyst's 'low' to 'medium' in a single year.

This organic acid releases the minerals even from insoluble rock; it is one of the ways in which plants first built up soil out of the primeval inorganic world and, together with roots that go down far below the soil analyst's auger, is the reason why organic farming no more exhausts the land than growing oaks for 5,000 years in the same wood. Because plants are efficient gatherers of what they need, they often acquire minerals where in theory there are none. Lupins and lucerne can both gather zinc; the cabbage is greedy for sulphur; bracken obtains potash on potash-deficient land; and the nettle extracts lime from an acid soil, not by a mysterious power, but merely by searching a far wider area than any soil sampling and for a longer time.

Of the fifty or sixty minerals which have been found in plants, and which are present mainly in an insoluble form in the soil, not all have been proved to be essential to their growth, health and nutrition. Those which have proved to be so include: boron, calcium, chlorine, copper, fluorine, magnesium, manganese, molybdenum, nickel, silicon and zinc. Many of these minerals are present only in minute quantities in a fertile soil and, on this 'drop in the ocean' basis, are required by plants and animals. The point to remember about these so-called 'trace elements' is, that a healthy soil contains only a trace of them; provide more than this and you will get no return for your money or the element is actively harmful; 0·01 parts per million of boron can cause deficiency symptoms, whilst 1·0 p.p.m. can be toxic to certain plants. Organic matter acts as a buffer against both over- and under-supply.

By returning to the soil organic matter containing the equivalent quantities of minerals to those removed in crops, by keeping in motion the processes by which more of these essential plant foods are released from the soil's store and by using, in a rotation, deep-rooting plants which delve straight into the untapped vaults at lower soil levels, the organic gardener on fertile soil ensures a continuous supply of minerals of all kinds. Many organic gardeners have remedied deficiencies of minerals in an available form, revealed by analysis and poor crops, merely by securing a quicker turn-over. In extreme cases, such as the total absence of cobalt and magnesium from certain fen soils and others, inorganic chemicals may be the only quick and economic means of obtaining a crop, but these are exceptions. Far more often, trace element and other shortages are the 'bank charges' of orthodox soil management of which chemistry is the cashier. Until very recently, not even the most compound of 'artificial' fertilizers contained trace elements. But the inclusion of minute quantities of trace elements in the chemist's mixed bag of chemical fertilizers can lead to an alarming danger. These trace elements may never break down in the soil. They are there for ever. As and when more, regular fertilizer applications are made year after year so a build-up of trace elements in the soil occurs. A steady build-up will most certainly lead to a toxic condition and field upon field, garden upon garden may be unable to sustain plant life. This pessimistic shadow is but one of the fears the organic gardener has for the future of mankind on this planet. Will mankind destroy itself in this way? The atomic bomb is one nightmare the chemist gave us. A greater nightmare is the dead hand of the chemist on the shallow soil of our planet.

Calcium, one of the minerals, is essential to green plants and all animals, though it is not required by fungi and some of the lower algae. Calcium in the form of calcium carbonate (chalk) is present in the decayed organic matter of the compost heap. Fair amounts of lime are therefore added to the garden soil when garden compost is applied to it. A soil which is dressed generously with garden compost is invariably the home of a multitude of earthworms and there is normally three times as much available calcium in earthworm casts as there is in the surrounding soil. Large quantities are also brought into circulation by some plants, such as buckwheat and broom, and nettle foliage is rich in calcium even when this weed grows where few others will, in the markedly acid soil surrounding the backyard chicken run. By means of these combined processes, sufficient calcium may be released in the soil of the established organic garden to eliminate altogether the necessity for application of lime, either as a fertilizer or as an acid-neutralizer.

The relative acidity or alkalinity of a medium is measured by what is called a scale of pH. In this scale, pH 7·0 denotes neutrality, figures lower than this acidity and higher figures alkalinity. As the scale is logarithmic, pH 5·0 denotes ten times the acidity of pH 6·0, and pH 9·0 ten times the alkalinity of pH 8·0. (Incidentally, vinegar has a pH of about 2·5, lemon juice 2·6, beer between 5·0 and 6·0, fresh milk 6·5 and caustic soda 9·5.) In Britain we have no soils of a reaction above pH 8·5 or below pH 4·0, but extremes of either acidity or alkalinity within these limits can cause trouble. Liming in excess, to enable plants to draw on the soil's 'bank balance', traditionally 'makes both farm and farmer poor'. Too much calcium locks up potash and some other minerals and demonstrates the need for large quantities of organic matter on calcareous soils. Some plants will not flourish on an acid soil (often by reason of this non-availability of certain minerals essential to them), whilst *Plasmodiophora brassicae*, the organism which causes club-root disease of brassicas, prefers it. Practically all of our crop plants flourish best in a near-neutral soil, neither too acid nor too alkaline, and the same applies to most of the organisms populating the soil (although there are exceptions).

Apart from the organisms which juggle with nitrogen and those which help to make 'major' and 'trace' minerals available to plants, there are others which break down cellulose and organic matter in general and also various 'specialist' bacteria. In this last category is the amazing *Thiobacillus thio-oxidans*, which disintegrates and converts sulphur to sulphuric acids. The gardener who puts fresh coal ashes on the vegetable plot raises a dense crop of this organism which, when fed with unlimited sulphur, will, in theory, bring a soil down to pH 1·0—despite liming. Though this bacterium cannot economically be used to replace the chemical factory in supplying accumulator acid, it has been used in America to reclaim alkali deserts spread with sulphur wastes—as a sort of inverted liming.

All this goes to prove that the life of the soil is not a philosophical abstraction, but an immensely complex, interlocking world of ever-changing species of living creatures, rising and falling in numbers with varying conditions of moisture, acidity or alkalinity, and food supply. Many of the smaller creatures are transparent and need to be stained before they can be seen, even under a high-powered microscope. Most are so small that they can live in the moisture film that clings to soil particles as though swimming in a sea. Although we know a great deal about them, this is surprisingly little compared to what there is still to be discovered.

The 'currency exchange' operated by the soil population, and to a lesser extent also by plants, is largely ignored under orthodox systems of soil management. The major nutrients, the familiar N, P and K, and (more recently) a few other minerals and growth-promoting substances, are added to the soil mainly in a form in which they are immediately available to plants. What is thus added goes (or is intended to go) to 'current account' for immediate spending, to secure an increased yield in the shortest space of time. But the 'bank charges' are sometimes obvious and heavy. The artificial supply of potash does not seem to fit root systems designed and adapted to take this mineral in other ways. Seventy per cent of the value of sulphate of ammonia may be washed down field drains, apart from the quantity of good lime it converts to useless gypsum (calcium sulphate). Of the minerals and other elements removed from the land in crop after crop, only a few of those known to be necessary are returned in the form of fertilizers or manures, therefore deficiencies frequently occur. It is from those gardeners and farmers who return no organic matter to continuously cropped soils that the highest 'bank charges' are levied. That 'artificial' plant foods do not eliminate the need for organic matter has been stressed repeatedly by soil scientists. Unfortunately, their pronouncements do not pack the punch of advertisements concerned with the sale (but not necessarily the correct use) of usually high-priced commodities. It is at least in part the 'misuse' of 'artificial' fertilizers that has resulted in a complete revision of principles and techniques by organic gardeners and farmers.

The aims of organic cultivation are to secure the advantages and economies of working with nature, by the same general methods, to bring more and more plant foods into circulation and to obtain the greatest yields of the most nutritious crops whilst maintaining the fertility of the soil. As soil organisms require longer than can always be afforded, especially under intensive methods of cultivation, for the release of plant foods and the decomposition of organic matter allowed to die back naturally into the soil, the organic cultivator mainly starts these processes outside the soil by the quick, 'factory' process of composting.

In its modern form, the technique of composting, and of organic gardening generally, is far younger than that of lawn-cutting by motor mower (1905; the first lawn mower was invented by William Budding in 1831), though it is based on methods which have sustained the high yields of Chinese agriculture for the past forty centuries. It is essentially a method of microbiological 'farming' and the key to a system of getting the best out of both ancient and modern worlds, by speeding up the process of decomposition, by natural means, partly at high temperatures which reap incidental dividends in weed seeds and disease organisms cooked like grains of rice, and nitrogen fixed from the air. Although, when measured by laboratory techniques, the plant foods supplied in well-made compost are apparently the same as those supplied 'out of the bag', they are in the right concentration, in available and unavailable forms, and in the complexity which nature encourages but simple inorganic compounds do not provide. Perhaps even more important, they are accompanied by immense numbers of beneficial organisms. The good compost heap is vastly different from the smelly, weed-ridden rubbish dump seen in many kitchen gardens. As a gardening term, the word 'compost' has two meanings. The product of the compost heap is garden compost, often shortened to 'compost'. There are also propagating composts. Although sieved garden compost is itself an excellent propagating compost for many plant subjects most propagating composts are mixtures of peat, sand, loam and plant foods. There are also soil-less propagating composts. Unless something is said to the contrary, the word compost in this book is applied solely to garden compost.

The Indore compost heap (evolved by the late Sir Albert Howard at the Indore Research Station in India, and modified forms of which are recommended throughout this book) consists of a series of layers of mixed vegetable matter, with between them other layers of organic nitrogenous manure (the 'activator') and yet others of chalk, limestone, earth or wood ash (the 'neutralizer' or 'base'), lightly built, and moistened if necessary.

The mixed materials of which the Indore compost heap is made contain a certain amount of nitrogen. Young, fresh, green plant wastes may contain up to 2 per cent, but there may be as little as $\frac{1}{2}$ of 1 per cent in tough, mature stems. But nitrogen is required in a proportion between 1·2–3 and 1·8 per cent, on a dry weight basis, of the total carbohydrates, as energy food for fungi and bacteria in the heap. (Phosphates and trace elements are also required but these are commonly found in sufficient quantity in the materials to be composted.) We add the extra nitrogen in the form of dung, urine, dried blood or other organic manures. (The need for this nitrogen in the compost heap is demonstrated very forcibly by the slow decay of a pile of dead leaves. These are mostly hard and woody skeletons: cellulose, hemicelluloses (tougher still) and lignin (most resistant of all), with only a very little of the quickly-rotted carbohydrates. Though a pile steams and shrinks a little, it becomes with age a solid mass like plug tobacco, valuable as a moisture-retaining sponge and source of slowly available plant foods, but of little use as a quick-acting, rich manure.) In a well-aerated compost heap, the organisms which break down organic matter to the carbon dioxide and water, free nitrogen and simple elements, the wasters of the plant foods in a normal manure heap are kept at a minimum, and those which gather nitrogen and leave the greatest amount of plant foods and decayed organic matter ready to take into circulation again, are favoured. The Indore heap begins with roughly 30 parts of carbon in woody matter and carbohydrates to between 1 and 2 parts of nitrogen in the manure or 'activator'. At the end of the composting process, the carbon/nitrogen ratio may be about 10/1, so that, unlike raw organic matter, mature compost can be cultivated in without soil robbery of nitrogen (such as occurs when organisms deal with excess carbon-containing matter) and without loss of nitrogen or humus (such as occurs when highly-nitrogenous manures are buried). Most of the difference goes in providing the heat. The air throughout the lightly-built compost heap provides the oxygen required by aerobic fungi and bacteria to break down the carbon compounds to carbon dioxide again, releasing energy in the slow combustion on which all life from bacteria to Olympic athletes depends for power. Some of the difference is due to the fact that there is more nitrogen in the heap than when it was built. The late Sir Albert Howard held the record with a gain of 26 per cent more combined nitrogen than went into one Indore heap, in vegetable waste and activator; 15 per cent of nitrogen is a common gain, by *Azotobacter* which multiply in certain outside portions of the heap during the final stage of composting.

The nitrogen fixed from the air and released from decaying organic matter in the compost heap and in the soil to which compost is applied, provides for the organic gardener the equivalent of the chemical expensively bought in by the orthodox to replace that which is wasted under normal methods of cultivation and manure-making. In addition, other plant foods otherwise locked up in the woody matter of the materials or highly concentrated and easily washed out in the familiar black pools of the rain-soaked farmyard, are still in the heap in a highly available form.

Air is necessary for the respiration of the beneficial fungi and bacteria, including the nitrogen-fixing *Azotobacter* and the cellulose-decomposing bacteria. The reign of these is short in the mass of over-wet dung in the farmyard manure pile. The need for air is further demonstrated when double-trenching, as it so often does, reveals vegetable matter almost unchanged some months after having been dug into the lower levels of the soil. When water, and available nitrogen are present, but air is excluded from an over-compact compost heap, organisms obtain their oxygen from the organic compounds of the decaying materials which are then reduced to smelly sulphur and nitrogen compounds: putrefied. Sufficient air (circulated inward and upwards) throughout the compost heap is ensured by lightly building this on a fibrous stack bottom (made of such materials as large prunings, bracken and straw, etc.) or over a 'herring-bone' of half drain pipes, by intimately mixing together materials of different texture so that they do not 'bind' and by making vertical ventilation holes to its base. The excessive aeration which drives away heat, also the cooling effects of winds and rains, are avoided by giving the compost heap protection by building it in a bin. Protection is also afforded a heap by draping it with sacks, rugs, carpets and discarded clothing. These coverings look ugly and at one time an additional cover—a tarpaulin sheet—was advised. But sacks and other organic covers (including tarpaulin) gradually rot down, too, during the fermentation process. A newer final covering suggested for compost heaps is 500-gauge black polythene. There are fairly wide limits between good and bad aeration of the compost heap and experience indicates the sort of building that is most successful.

Moisture is necessary for decay and as a means of transportation for micro-organisms. A haystack is an example of dead vegetable matter *preserved* by dryness. If it is not quite dry enough, an amazing succession of warmth-loving *thermophils* take over, in the end create the bacterial equivalent to atomic warfare and char or set light to the heap. Too much moisture leaches valuable nutrients, prevents free circulation of air, and cools the compost heap—in which the moisture content aimed at is 45 to 50 per cent or slightly more (Sir Albert Howard's famous 'consistency of a squeezed-out sponge'). Some waterlogged materials, such as fresh seaweed, require to be drained, others, such as fresh lawn mowings or Russian Comfrey foliage, require to be wilted for a few hours, when used in bulk for compost-making. A ton of straw, on the other hand, has to be soaked with roughly 800 gallons of water if 'composted' by the method described in Chapter IV. The mixed materials of the Indore heap usually need only to be lightly moistened.

WHY ORGANIC GARDENING?

It is not possible (and might not be desirable) to exclude from the compost heap any particular one of the many races of fungi and bacteria which are present everywhere, in dust, soil, air and organic matter. Most of this microscopic life prefers a near-neutral medium, as do most of our cultivated plants. The maximum acidity tolerated by the *Azotobacter* is pH 5·6, and by the cellulose-decomposing bacteria 6·4. (This is the reason why peat moors are poor in nitrogen and cannot break down but often build up as much as 15 feet of humus, of use only as fuel.) Both types of bacteria are most active between pH 7·0 and 8·0. During the process of decomposition of organic matter, fungi and bacteria release weak organic acids which, if allowed to accumulate, would inhibit or arrest decay. This is illustrated in a heap of lawn mowings which is both damp and rich in the most readily-decayed ingredients: starches, sugars and proteins. It is attacked by fungi and bacteria within a few hours, and becomes amazingly hot inside for a brief period, but the mounting acidity of the process (and the absence of air) prevents aerobic decomposition and causes putrefaction. The resultant slimey, fermented mass, applied to the land—except in the bottom of a pea trench where the root-nodule bacteria of these leguminous plants will take care of their nitrogen requirements—can produce a drastic fall in crop yield. This acidifying process is, of course, exploited in the silage pit. Here, deliberate exclusion of air and the addition of diluted treacle produce bacterial action of a type which results, in this case, in a long-keeping and highly nutritious 'vegetable cheese'.

In theory, carbonic acid is the only acid produced in the well-aerated compost heap of mixed vegetable wastes, but in practice many humic acids are formed. A proportion of old compost is probably the best neutralizer because, in addition to its free bases, it contains minerals and immense numbers of organisms which usefully 'innoculate' the heap. A close second is earth, of which enough usually gets into the heap on the roots of weeds and plants. However, the ground chalk or limestone which, when added to the Indore heap, keeps the pH between 7·2 and 7·7 (rising with age), justifies itself both in theory and practice for the first few years, although the third-year organic gardener can often compost without it.

Knowledge of organic husbandry is based mainly on results, which is why this book is concerned mainly with practice. Explanations are often hidden or shrouded in the vast bulk of the unknown. So far, no integrated research team has ever followed, step by step, the bacteriological and fungicidal changes in population under various methods of composting—an immensely expensive task which no research station has ever had the funds to tackle. In a general sense, the behaviour of organisms in a compost heap has, therefore, to be judged in the same way as rush hours for London tube trains: probability gauged by experience.

Soon after the compost heap is made, the temperature rises as fungi, bacteria and protozoa attack the carbohydrates and proteins of the vegetable matter and oxidation results in the liberation of energy in the form of heat. The temperature rise may be slow and accomplished in part by the slower-growing fungi if the materials in the heap are all or mainly tough or mature, or if there is insufficient nitrogen. It may be fast, if there is much fresh green material, such as lawn mowings, which consist in part of readily-available proteins and carbohydrates, and within a day or so rocket the heap into top gear at temperatures between 130° and 180° F. (55° and 83° C.). At this point, the fungi and bacteria which start the heating process are mainly replaced by the few specialized types of *thermophils* (warmth-lovers) and actinomycetes which are active at high temperatures and which continue to attack proteins and carbohydrates, including some of the more resistant ones. These organisms may continue to 'work', and the heap temperature to persist at 113–120° F. (45–49° C.), for well over a month. As food supplies diminish, the temperature of the heap slowly falls and the *thermophils* are replaced by immense numbers of those organisms which flourish at more normal temperatures and whose numbers only very slowly decline after the heap reaches outside air temperature. Some of these attack pathogenic (disease-producing) organisms which have survived the high temperature phase; some of the cannibalistic nematodes feed on saprophytic and parasitic species such as eelworms; yet other nematodes; consume bacteria, fungi and organic matter and some fungi feed on the nematodes. Some organisms synthesize vitamins (which are in part decomposed by others), produce growth-promoting substances and antibiotics—the latter of which may be a potent factor in the marked disease-resistance of organically-grown crops.

The compost heap brings into circulation nutrients from waste organic matter which all too often goes up in smoke on garden bonfires, is pushed into the dustbin or is carried in the boot of the car for dumping on waste land or in hedgerows. Composted wastes supply a large volume of nutrients in available form, and in the protoplasm of the immense numbers of fungi and bacteria which accompany compost when it is applied to the soil, and an annuity of these slowly released from incompletely decayed fractions of organic matter. It carries food for many future generations of organisms, including earthworms, and supplies humus, the natural 'conditioner' of the soil. Compost does not consist entirely of humus, which, in the scientific sense, is the end-product of plant constituents, such as lignin, extremely resistant to decay and of little use as food for organisms—although it can be used if nothing else is available. The value of humus lies in its water-holding capacity and coagulating effects on the soil; only a portion of the value of compost lies in its content of humus.

Organic gardening, of which the use of compost is a part, may be the answer to problems seemingly insoluble from any other view-point. In the garden, on the allotment and in horticulture in general, compost is definitely the answer to the scarcity and high cost of organic manures. Waste organic matter, including household refuse and any of the materials mentioned individually in Chapter III (indeed, in a general sense, any that were once 'living'), added in the form of compost, can enable even the poorest of soils to be built up to a high state of fertility, where advantages of flavour and quality in produce are at their highest. Compost, as will be seen later, can also be a potent factor in the arresting of disease, including troubles, such as hookworm, which are a scourge of mankind in a hot climate. The objection is often made that in the East, where composting began, health standards are lower for certain diseases than in the Western world, but it is unfair, to say the least, to attribute to a traditional composting method, the results mainly of a lack of knowledge of hygiene and antiseptics and starvation from flooding and economic evils.

Compost, alone, is neither a cure-all nor a substitute for skill, and a failure in orthodox gardening will be a failure in organic gardening.

How far compost pays (in the short view) in cash on a nursery or market garden, depends on how good a composter the gardener is, and on his ingenuity in evolving time and labour-saving methods.

CHAPTER II

COMPOSTING METHODS

C ompost-making is an art, a branch of gardening which deserves the same attention and skill as the old arts of brewing, baking and cheese-making, all of which apply biological principles. Once its technique has been mastered, it takes no more time to do it really well than to make an inferior product.

The Modified Indore Compost Heap for the Small Garden

Site selection of the small heap (which is all the town gardener or allotment holder can manage at one time) is mainly for convenience, economy on crop-producing space and the saving of labour in making and handling compost which weighs out at about a cubic yard and a half to the ton. It depends on both the garden and the gardener. To place a heap in the right- or left-hand corner of the garden on sloping ground, makes for easy turning and barrowing of compost downhill, whilst labour can often be saved in the collection of raw materials (which, although lighter to handle, take more space than the finished product in the barrow) if the heap-site is in the middle of the garden —at the path side so that the composter does not have to tread over wet ground when periodically adding extra material to the heap. Often the only way to make sure of getting all kitchen scraps is to place the heap so near to the house that the contents of the sink pan and the vacuum cleaner have to be carried to it not much farther than they otherwise would be to the fire or the dustbin—an important point for the elderly composter. Alternatively, have a light metal or plastic bin (with a lid) near the kitchen door. Place all household wastes in the bin as and when they are collected. Keep the lid on the bin so that flies do not enter. Empty the bin on to the compost heap at least once each week. Wash out the bin and return it to the kitchen door.

28

COMPOSTING METHODS

For general soil improvement in the garden successive heaps can be placed in different parts of it provided that they are near a path. The loss of the small area out of commission for three months or so under each heap is rarely serious because of the greater cropping-capacity of organically managed soils.

In a windy garden a windbreak (usually on the north side) is needed particularly by the slow-heating autumn-made heap, in which every degree above outside air temperature has to be fought for against the cooling effects of wind and rain. To keep off the fierce winds which cause most serious heat losses and to hide the heap (although, if correctly built, it need be no less tidy than a cold frame), make use of existing shrubs or bushes, and sacking or wickerwork fences. Put up a windbreak if none exists, but choose a productive one; beware of privet which requires constant cutting if it is to be kept tidy and produces nothing more valuable than foliage. To place the compost heap behind a good stand of raspberry canes or currant bushes is to obtain a dividend of high-quality fruit as well as valuable weather protection. The best place for the heap in a really exposed garden may be in the angle of the garden wall (which then forms two sides of a 'bin'), or under the branch canopy of an overhanging fruit tree. However, it is best not to place a heap directly under the drip-line of overhanging branches, where it is liable to be over-moistened by the rain that normally goes straight to the farthest-reaching capillary roots. Moisture is necessary for decay, but not in this quantity, nor in the douche of water which comes from the unguttered roof of the potting shed on a wet day. These observations do not apply if the heap is protected by a tarpaulin or black polythene sheet.

A permanent composting site should be out of the wind and out of the way (all other considerations being equal), also high and dry, not in a depression where surface drainage collects and will give the heap a cold foot-bath every time rain falls. A dry, porous foundation is essential as heaps are built directly on bare ground to allow free access to micro-organisms and earthworms. Soil needs no preparation or can be lightly forked over, but turf should be inverted to prevent the formation of an acid layer which might keep earthworms and other organisms out of the heap. If the site is on heavy clay, it pays to take out a 6- to 8-inch depth of this and to replace half the quantity on top of a layer of sand, gravel or rubble, filled into the hole to improve drainage. Concrete is unsuitable as a site foundation for the small heap; it insulates this from the earth, cools it somewhat and prevents free drainage.

The minimum successful size for a compost heap is a 4-foot cube. The heap up to 5 feet square and high is practically all 'outsides' and is susceptible to weather fluctuations, it is therefore built in a pit or bin, the main objects of which are heat-insulation, weather-protection and tidiness. (The larger heap—dealt with in the second section of this chapter—survives without protection because of its lower ratio of outer surface to internal capacity and because of the higher temperatures generated in it.)

A round or rectangular pit on a permanent site wins hands down for cheapness, although it involves a little heavy labour when first constructed. It should be dug at least 4 feet across, but of any length, 18 inches to 2 feet deep (not more or air will be kept out), its sides sloped slightly inward towards the bottom. The excavated soil, stacked and trodden round its edges to form a lip or wall, gives the pit a depth of about 3 feet to 3 ft. 6 in. and prevents the run-in of surface drainage water. If the surrounding soil is fine and loose, the pit walls should be reinforced with packed clay, loose stones, bricks or fibrous turves (which break down well, here, for use in potting mixtures). Inverted turves should also be used, where possible, to cover the bottom of the pit, like paving stones. Loose rubble will do as an alternative to form the solid lining which prevents the deepening and widening of the pit every time compost is removed—when it is sometimes difficult to tell where composted materials end and the pit walls and bottom begin.

The main advantages of pit composting are the uniform breakdown which is brought about by greater heat-retention than the bin gives, and direct contact between composted materials and the surrounding earth (to which earthworms retire whilst the heap is at its hottest). Turning is avoided, as only the top layer of a few inches of the heap is left undecayed after three months, and this is easily stripped off and added to the next heap or used as the foundation of it. Practically anything can be put into the pit; perennial weed roots rarely survive composting below the surface, and watering is reduced to a minimum. The biggest snag when composting underground in a wet or low-lying area is the danger of waterlogging, which occurs if the water-table rises near the surface and the pit half floods from below. To make sure of getting compost and not swill, from a hole which can be an early grave for valuable vegetable matter, and also because the pit must stay put, it should be carefully sited. A bin will

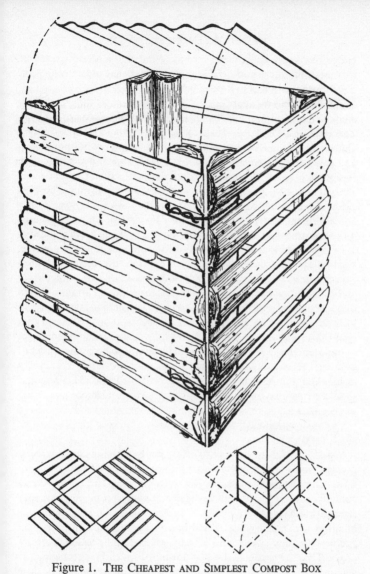

Figure 1. THE CHEAPEST AND SIMPLEST COMPOST BOX

The materials required are, offcuts, screws or nails, some thick wire (for 'twists' to secure corners) and corrugated iron or wood (to form a sloping roof). It can be made from 4 to 5 feet in size, each way, and be assembled in a few seconds.

budge, however, and can be moved round the garden in rotation, tried here and there until trial and error experience indicates the best permanent site and is first-class for tidiness.

Few horticultural suppliers stock compost bins as the demand for them is small, but obtainable in some places are versions of the New Zealand Compost Bin, designed by the New Zealand Humic Compost Club. The essential features of any bin or enclosure are bottomlessness and at least one detachable or removable side so that materials can be forked in, turned if necessary, and the end-product be shovelled straight out into the barrow without unnecessary lifting. The New Zealand-type bin is easy to construct with a few off-cuts, some nails and a little ingenuity. A strong 5-foot packing case may also be used if the bottom is knocked out, the lid hinged to the top and wedged at the front to form a sloping roof and with one side made removable. Ventilation holes, each about 2 inches apart in rows at vertical intervals of 6 to 9 inches round the bin, can be made quickly with a brace and 2-inch bit, or by removing alternate side planks, splitting or sawing a couple of inches off their width and replacing them to give interstices like those in the New Zealand bin. Planks should not be less than an inch thick or more than about 5 feet long (the maximum length required), and need to be well protected against the decaying effects of weathering from outside, heat, moisture and micro-biological activity inside. Old sump oil is the best preservative for wooden bins and should be painted on thick after every fourth or fifth compost heap has been made and removed. Tar and creosote are unsuitable, as both inhibit micro-biological activity somewhat and keep earthworms at arm's length.

Wood is by far the best construction material to use, and any thick (uncreosoted) timber will do. Old railway sleepers (obtainable from most railway stores depots) are just the thing, piled two or three horizontally in the form of a three-sided rectangle (open-ended because sleepers are heavy to shift). Straw bales win over sleepers for ease of handling and management, for they can be assembled into a bay or enclosure of any size, round a heap which decomposes right to its edges. They are gradually broken down by rain and micro-biological activity, but, nevertheless, survive for several heaps; wires can then be cut and the partly decomposed straw added to the following heap —surrounded by new bales. Bins made of two thicknesses of tough wire netting, kept apart by a 6-inch filling of straw or sacks, stretched taut round four corner posts, last for a short time only, but are so

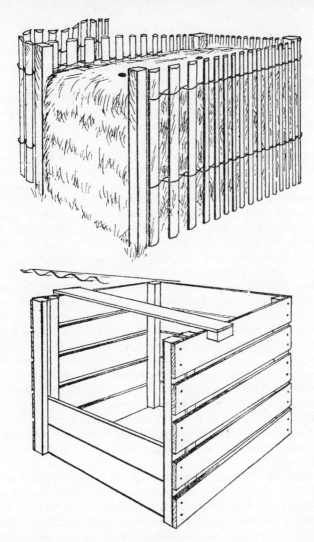

Figure 2

Above: an enclosure of split-chestnut fencing, stretched taut round four stout corner posts, can be draped with sacks and covered during the coldest, wettest months. Below: a bin of the 'New Zealand type'. The back and sides are permanently fixed. Removable boards can be slipped in or out at the front as the heap is being built up inside or dismantled.

light that they can be lifted bodily from the heap when the time arrives for compost to be turned or used. Although such temporary bins are useful for the first experimental heap, they are almost playthings to the experienced composter. Corrugated iron, used otherwise than as a sloping roof, weighted down with bricks or wood, does not effectively keep out the cold or let in sufficient air and inevitably corrodes and buckles, apart from being unsightly. Concrete is also unsuitable. During recent years several manufacturers have been advertising mesh fencing as a help in compost making. Metal meshes tend to rust unless they are well galvanized or coated with a rust-proof preventive. Netlon Garden Mesh is all plastic and should be long lasting. Several stout stakes need to be hammered into the ground and the Netlon mesh (2-inch gauge) tied securely to them. With all sorts of mesh there is the objection that much heat is lost from the sides of the heap. This loss of heat may be prevented by lining the sides with several sheets of damp newsprint, card or even with damp straw. These linings, being organic, will of course rot down with the heap. When the heap is being dug out there is no need to remove the stakes. But, of course, remove the Netlon mesh.

Apart from the fact that a bin made of wood or of plastic mesh assists in retaining heat generated within a compost heap there are two other points in favour of bins. It can be extremely difficult to keep the sides of a heap absolutely straight and upright at an angle of 90 degrees where a heap is not being made in a bin. This means that the top of the heap is often small and the heap resembles a pyramid. Being far smaller in total volume than was intended, the heap does not heat up nor retain its heat for long. Tidiness is most necessary in the garden and heaps made in bins are tidier than those built without retaining walls.

A pit or bin of the 3- to 5-foot size will usually take the waste portions of crops, weeds and kitchen scraps collected over a period of about a month by the allotment holder or town gardener new to composting. The country composter, on the same scale, usually needs two bins of the 5-foot size, to take materials which can be collected with less selection than for rabbit feed as any greenstuff will do. At least two bins of the large size are needed on the quarter-acre garden. If it is not possible to build a 6-foot heap in one operation, a second bin or pit is always useful, for two heaps, built independently but at the same time, can be 'potted on' into a single one, at the turning or for final maturing, to leave one bin ready to take the new heap. The best heap is usually built in a single operation, so that two small bins, either of which can be filled 'in one go', are better than one which takes several weeks to be filled, two can be placed side by side, or four arranged like the sections of Battenburg cake, for heat exchange, added weather protection and tidiness.

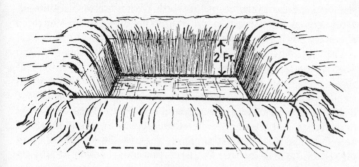

Figure 3

The compost pit, dug 2 feet deep, 4 to 6 feet wide and of any length greater than this, is made deeper by the stacking of excavated soil and turves round its edges to form a wall or 'lip'.

A clean site with tidy heaps is the place to start the control of all pests on the organic garden. A litter of decaying vegetation and a good stand of weeds is an open invitation to slugs to come and lay their eggs in a cool heap. Most of these pests, the worst in a wet area, are kept away by a weed-free 'no-man's-land' of about a foot round each heap, so the heap site should be kept clean. Sawdust is a good slug deterrent, will keep the heap-surround dry, clean and weed-free, and the preliminary weathering it gets will help with quicker break-down of this resistant material when it is collected and composted— as it should be about once a year.

Where the compost is to be made in a pit or where the heap is going to be much larger than is usual it is advisable to have a rough founda-tion. The purpose of this is to admit to the heap the air that is required by aerobic organisms which ferment the wastes in the heap. This 6-inch foundation is a good place in which to deal with much tough stuff that would have to be well chopped up beforehand and would take longer than most ordinary heap ingredients to break down. It can consist of old pea or bean sticks, maize or sunflower stalks, thick prunings of non-prickly subjects, brushwood, bracken, brussels sprouts stems— in fact anything that will admit air. Large heaps and pits of any size need ventilation holes, too. A smallish pit needs but one; large heaps need one hole for every square yard of surface. Easiest way of making a ventilation hole is by pushing a crowbar through from the top until the ground beneath the heap is reached. With smallish garden heaps the retention of heat within the heap is the aim. No foundation is necessary nor is there any need for a ventilation hole.

The vegetable material which will form the main part of the compost heap, can be collected on 365 days of the year. Crop residues such as pea, bean, tomato and potato haulm, leaves, lawn mowings, small twigs and fine hedge clippings, spent flowers, vacuum cleaner dust, cigarette butts, coffee grounds and tea leaves, egg shells, small or torn rags, odd bits of paper—in fact, practically anything that has once lived and most of what ordinarily goes into the dustbin or on to the bonfire—will be suitable. Weeds are first class; as many as possible should be caught before seeds have set and, with any diseased foliage, for extra safety, can be put well into the centre of the heap. Milk bottle tops, toothpaste tubes, razor blades and odd bits of metal should not go in. Some other unsuitable materials are mentioned in Chapter III. The greater the variety of suitable stuff the better; it is little use trying to make compost with only frosted foliage and a week's collection of newspapers. Most vegetable wastes will be available for composting during the warmer months, from late February or March when the first weeds are cleared from the seed-bed and can be mixed with winter-stored scraps, until late October to take the final revenue of leaves, frosted dahlia foliage and the woody stems of the herbaceous border. But compost-making should be a continuous process, like painting the Forth Bridge, and a period as intense as is jam-making when fruit is plentiful, should be made to coincide with the harvesting of quick-maturing crops, grown to provide compost material instead of green manure for cultivating in by normal methods. Many annuals, such as garden and field lupins, can be sown for flowers as well as fertility, after early crops are off the garden; perennial Russian Comfrey (*Symphytum peregrinum*) can be established on, round or even in the chicken run, or on the waste patch where nothing else will flourish, to provide, from the second year onwards, six to eight cuts a year of readily decayed greenstuff. A friendly greengrocer may often have vegetable wastes for your compost heaps and your butcher may have used sawdust. Pigeon fanciers seem always on the look-out for a gardener who will take away sacks of droppings. In many small gardens there is often manure from cages housing pet rabbits or hamsters. This manure is destined for the garbage bin unless you collect it. It is fashionable to have a lawn but here again many lawn owners have an excess of grass clippings which they are eager to dispose of to you and to other compost-minded gardeners. In tree-lined streets there are leaves aplenty in late autumn and some parks or highways departments are willing to deliver loads of fallen leaves to gardeners. Autumn leaves are best stacked and covered with a sheet of 500-gauge black polythene where they will decay gradually. Autumn leaves can be used as mulches provided that your garden is not near slug-infested land. Slugs will trek from such land and take up abode beneath the leaves and feed at night on your garden plants. Offers of lawn mowings from bowling greens, golf courses and parks should be considered. Ask if unpleasant chemicals have been used to stimulate growth of the grass or if selective weedkillers have been used. Refuse offers of chemical-contaminated mowings. Local factories processing foods may have wastes for your compost heaps. The keen organic gardener is always on the look-out for sources of raw materials for the compost heap.

The compost heap usually consists of 75 per cent or more of vegetable matter, plus activator and neutralizer. For the small heap it can help if all the ingredients are mixed thoroughly, and watered if they are dry, before stacking the mixture in a pit or bin. The object of pre-mixing is to get a uniform mixture of tough materials with those more readily decayed, moist with dry, thick with thin, young with old; to avoid thick layers or forkfuls of sawdust, or such materials which 'blanket' or pack and insulate one part of the heap from another, and to eliminate air pockets which cause uneven decomposition. The organic gardener's brussels sprouts' stalks and other long stems not used in the heap foundation and too big to go in the 4-foot heap as they are, can be chopped into short lengths for easier handling and quicker breakdown (although they can easily be put through second or third heaps if they fail to decompose by the time other ingredients have done so). The rubber-wheeled traffic of the English garden does not give sufficient pressure, but on a hard surface the iron garden roller will do the same job as Sir Albert Howard's bullock carts, crushing sann hemp spread on the roads surrounding the composting site at Indore. There is little point in chopping or crushing the ordinary revenue of weeds and kitchen wastes (although it makes for much quicker compost-production). Pre-mixing can, of course, be started in the chicken run, managed on 'deep litter' lines, or the pig pen into which all waste vegetable matter is thrown.

Chemical activators or proprietary ones with secret ingredients (even though they may have an 'organic base') should be avoided, but this does not limit selection from several. Any sort of animal manure is suitable; so also are some organic manures such as dried blood. The packeted herbal activator (mentioned in Appendix I) is extremely useful in towns where access to the garden is through the ground floor or basement of a house and manure-carrying through the sitting-room isn't popular. Wherever there is a garden, there is a gardener; a return to the chamber-pot in towns, and the earth closet in country districts, would yield a constant supply of the best possible activator. Urine, diluted to a colourless liquid with about twenty times the quantity of water, provides activator and moisture in one go, and, like faeces, loses all repellent characteristics in the heap. The quantity required of any given activator depends on its nitrogen content. Farmyard manure should be used at the rate of about a quarter by bulk of the total vegetable matter in the heap, fresh poultry manure at one-twenty-fourth, and the herbal activator homeopathically. In practice, it is better to use too little than too much of any activator, thus avoiding the losses from leaching and gaseous dispersal that occur when there is an excess of nitrogen. Least activator of all is required if the heap consists of plenty of young, green, nitrogen-rich foliage.

The quantity of 'base' or acid neutralizer required is small. If ground chalk or limestone is used, 1 to 2 per cent (by bulk of the vegetable wastes in the heap) or about a double handful to every barrow-load, is sufficient to keep the pH reaction at its most favourable for beneficial organisms. The best neutralizers, old compost, and a very little good earth (if some has not been brought in on weed and crop roots) or a mixture of these and wood ashes, chalk or limestone, which bring in minerals and other elements, are useful in conserving nitrogen gas and inoculating the heap with micro-organisms.

Where the gardener decides to pre-mix instead of building a compost heap in layers, the three main ingredients of the heap—a good variety of vegetable wastes, activator and neutralizer—should be shaken with a fork so that they become well mixed together. If the mixture is very dry, it should be moistened through a rose can (preferably with water from the rain-butt rather than the tap), now or as the heap is built up, but never so generously as to cause water to run from the base. Watering is unnecessary if more than 50 to 60 per cent of the heap consists of fresh green materials. If more than 80 per cent, there is often less danger of faulty aeration if the vegetable wastes are wilted for a few hours to reduce their moisture content. Generally, all materials should be used as fresh as possible; a little rough stuff, twigs or straw, will prevent too-close packing. To pre-soak straw and hay in water for 48 hours or so, and thoroughly to wet paper or rags, is to bring these dry or slowly absorbent materials up to the 45 to 50 per cent moisture content which is necessary, and to prevent the slow decay, after several months, of a too-dry heap in which grey moulds take over and woodlice and ants find an ideal breeding and hunting ground.

The mixture, moistened if necessary, should then be stacked to a level with the top of the bin, or as much as a foot higher than the top of a pit. Discretion is needed when it comes to any firming of the heap. The ingredients of some heaps settle under their own weight; at other times a light firming with one's feet is called for. Excessive consolidation would exclude air. With a heap made out in the open and not in a bin a capping with an 'icing' is helpful in retaining heat within the heap. The 'icing' may be a 2-inch layer of manure topped with an equal depth of soil. Where so much manure is not to hand this covering may be soil. As has already been explained compost heaps made without the use of a bin are somewhat pyramidical in shape and the sloping sides can be coated with manure or soil provided that the soil is moist and has a fairly high clay content. If the heap is of a fair size use a pole to make a hole from top to bottom before sacking, discarded clothes, canvas, tarpaulin, polythene or any other covers are placed over the heap and held in position by lengths of scrap metal piping, house bricks or other weighty objects. Sufficient air for the good fermentation of the wastes reaches them because the covers do not in any sense lead to a heap being isolated from the atmosphere.

Trying to make good compost with materials which come from the kitchen in driblets of tea leaves, vegetable and fruit peelings, vacuum cleaner dust and string can be frustrating. This state of affairs is common in winter when few other wastes are around. Instead of starting a new heap with a weekly modicum of material it is better to store them until more and different wastes arrive on the scene. 'Storage' may be no more than covering the weekly household wastes with soil. Where cats or rats may dig out buried kitchen wastes they could be stored in a dustbin. Here again each layer needs covering with a little soil. But if the compost is being made in a pit then the weekly wastes may be emptied in, sprinkled with a little lime and some soil added to cover them.

Many gardeners prefer to build their compost heaps in separate layers. The pile starts off with a 6- to 8-inch layer of mixed vegetable wastes, lightly watered if necessary. The activator—manure, an organic manure-substitute or a proprietary product—is added. Some soil is then spread over the layer and a little ground chalk sprinkled over this to neutralize acidity. Layer upon layer is added sandwich-fashion either immediately or as and when more material becomes available. When the heap is from 4 feet to 5 feet high a light scatter of earth or old compost is then added, like sugar to a pie.

It is seldom possible to complete a heap at one operation and a partially built heap should be covered with sacking, an old carpet or coconut matting with the extra protection afforded by a sheet of black polythene, weighted down with poles or other weighty objects. This weatherproof and heat-retaining cover is removed as soon as more material is available and building continues with the addition of more layers in the same sequence as before (added like fuel to a fire), until the heap is of the required height. The essential of the method is to make at least a third of the heap at the first operation and not to let this cool down completely before the next consignment is added; if the temperature falls much below 100° F. (38° C.), added material will not heat up, or do so slowly (like fuel on a fire that has already died down). The best insurance against heat loss is to start off by making a full third of the heap, to add more layers within a week or a fortnight from the date of last building and to complete the heap in under six weeks (finishing off with manure and heat-insulator as before). Decomposition is rarely uniform in a heap built by this method, as the first layers get a head start over the final ones in decomposition, but a single turning a fortnight or three weeks after the final section is added gives a uniform mixture of fresh with part-decayed material. One of the advantages of this method of building in separate layers is, that seeded weeds and diseased foliage can be placed well in the centre of the heap, where there is likely to be the greatest kill because of highest temperatures, or be placed on the layers of lime or wood ash, the alkali in which also contributes to a clean end-product. The essential is to avoid thick layers of any one waste material, particularly leaves, coffee grounds, apple pomace, sawdust, etc. These and similar close-pack-

40

COMPOSTING METHODS

ing materials need to be scattered on to the heap in very thin layers, or be mixed with other vegetable wastes outside the heap before each layer is placed in position, if one part of the heap is not to be insulated from another.

The temperature-rise is swift in well-made spring and summer-built heaps, a large proportion of which consists of materials, such as lawn mowings, with plenty of readily decayed carbohydrates. Within the first week (later from autumn or winter building) temperatures between 130 and 160° F. (55 and 70° C.) can be registered on a special thermometer (or on the ordinary dairy variety suspended in a metal tube, plugged at one end to keep a clean, unbroken glass), by testing towards the centre and well down in the heap. However, temperature-testing by a method which comes into the same category as a bare elbow in the baby's bath water, is good enough for all but the mushroom grower, who makes a special compost, or the commercial man, who needs a very uniform, saleable commodity. If, at the end of the third week, a crowbar or a metal rod thrust for a couple of hours into the centre portion of the heap and to the bottom, comes out moist and too hot to hold, the composting process is going well; if it is cold and dry, it indicates that a turning should be given and water added; and if cold and wet (not just damp), that the heap is too moist and must be dried out. Even the smelliest ingredients, such as pig manure, should lose any individual smell by the day following that on which the heap is built—a constant source of wonder to the beginner. If an ammoniacal smell is given off, aeration is at fault or too much activator has been used. There should be no 'bad' smell and no fly-breeding. If the heap putrefies, due to excess moisture, acidity and lack of air, its value is not lost, but the only way to start off aerobic decomposition is to dismantle it wholly, reactivate and neutralize, and rebuild it with some additional dry, fibrous material such as straw or bracken. Need of moisture is indicated by dryness and failure of a heap to diminish in height during the first month; in such cases, more water should be added during the turning operation (or, if this is not given, by stripping off the top layer and moistening the heap with water from a rose can, or a slow hose, stuck into the sides of the heap at various points, but not left on to run for more than a few seconds). Poor fermentation of the well-protected heap usually indicates the need for extra nitrogen; the best activator for the high-cellulose autumn heap of slow-decaying, tough, fibrous stems, is poultry manure; this contains urea, broken down to ammonium carbonate, the form in which nitrogen is preferred by Hutchinson's *spirochaete*, one of the cellulose-decomposing bacteria which normally lives on straw. Often the autumn- or winter-built heap 'hangs fire' during frosty weather, when heat is spent in evaporating moisture and decay is slow because of tough materials and low air temperatures. If such a heap is left to over-winter, it will benefit by a turning in February or March, and be ready for the greater bacterial activity that warmer weather brings. Winter composting is tricky; although it can be managed with a good supply of poultry manure, it is better to store what little vegetable material there is at this time of the year and to use it for spring building.

The high temperatures, at which most weed seeds and disease organisms are killed, sometimes equal those in an electric soil sterilizer and are sustained for about three to four weeks, while the heap slowly settles on to its haunches and loses about a third of its original height. Gradually it cools to about 100 to 110° F. (38 to 43° C.) and, at the end of the fourth week, a turning should be given if a fairly fine end-product is required—and if there is sufficient labour.

The main object of turning is to bring to the inside of the re-made heap, for quicker breakdown, its cool and slow-decaying surface and sides, in which weed seeds and disease organisms might survive. The heap which contains many weeds, diseased foliage such as blighted tomato haulm and club-rooted brassica stems, or much tough material like sawdust, needs to be turned; so does the heap which is not built in one operation; also the heap, part or all of which is required for seed or potting mixtures.

Fine compost is generally best, or better, only for the quick-growing crops such as lettuces and radishes and for indoor work. Sieving of mature compost serves much the same purpose as (earlier) turning, to break down or eliminate fragments which would not go into a 10-inch pot or might give irregular germination, and takes less time ˙if only part of a heap is to be used when making up seed or potting mixtures. Sievings, put in the bottom of a seed tray, make good drainage material, or can be put through another compost heap. Little is otherwise gained by having a very fine-textured compost; rough stuff is excellent for potatoes, tomatoes and brassicas, and the rougher it is the better for stiff clay or sandy soil, on which fine compost is least successful as a texture improver for the first few years of organic cultivation. The surface cultivator likes a good proportion of rough stuff in his compost; it is applied where there is no danger of its causing nitrogen starvation; it gives undug soil maximum protection from rain and frost, provides food for fungi and bacteria during the winter and, because never completely or permanently wet, releases nutrients slowly over the complete growing season. For all these reasons, to turn the binned heap in which ingredients have been thoroughly mixed, or the pit-built heap in which breakdown is uniform apart from a thin surface layer, is usually considered as being unnecessary. The heap's undecomposed 'crust', which may contain many weed seeds, wind-blown or from dung dropped over-night by birds which come to the heap for warmth and shelter, can easily be split off with a fork and be put through another heap. Beneath the top 6 inches or so of dry stems and earth, breakdown is uniform, apart from any fragments of very rough material, such as tough or woody stems, which can easily be flicked out with a fork and put through another heap.

Thus, for ordinary garden use, a fairly rough compost is satisfactory, and can be obtained by carefully mixing ingredients before the heap is made, and by discarding the outer crust of the heap when this is broken down for use after three months or so. The easiest way to make a turning, necessary when fine material is required, or building was at fault, is to spade off the surface soil (for re-use on the next new heap) and to split down the heap from top to bottom in 6-inch widths, with a fork, just as when cutting bread. The partly decayed material can then be re-stacked in a second bin (or the same one removed bodily from around the heap before turning began), the outer crust carefully put into the centre of the new heap and ventilation holes made as before. During the turning operation, a little water should be added through a rose can or fine-nozzled hose if the heap has dried out by evaporation, but less than when the heap was first built. Too much moisture will keep out air, cause the decomposing material to 'pack', leach more readily available nutrients from it, and prevent the heap from getting its 'second wind'; a temperature usually well up to the 110° F. (43° C.) mark though rarely up to the sterilization point sometimes reached during the month before turning. The heap should never be quite dry (or breakdown is delayed), not sodden, or vegetable matter is cooled and may be broken down by putrefaction, instead of decomposition. At the turning, it is usually found that the moist vegetable matter in the heap is covered with a greyish-white fungal mycelium; this is one of the good signs, just as is the growth of toadstools on the heap-surface at a later stage.

The inside of the heap should begin to break down and darken in colour about ten days after the turning, that is, six to seven weeks from the date of building. A second turning can be given a fortnight or three weeks later if the whole heap is required for potting work. For the final phase of 'maturing', the heap can be re-stacked outside the bin if bin-space is needed; it needs no ventilation holes but should be well covered with sacking or black polythene.

Readiness of compost for ordinary use can be judged as the time when the heap is completely cold, and if, split down from top to bottom like cheese, it is easier handled with a spade than a fork; also by the presence of earthworms. There is no set time limit for the period from making to maturity, as the time required for the composting process varies with the climate, time of year, and materials used. In a temperate climate, compost is usually ready for ordinary use about ten to fifteen weeks after spring or summer building with a good proportion of fresh greenstuff (but a heap which takes twice the time to break down may be of similar quality). Sampled from the inside, beneath the surface crust, the mature heap resembles a forest humus or moist peat; 60 per cent of crumbly, moist compost may pass through a sieve with six meshes to the inch; it has a sweet earthy smell, a carbon/nitrogen ratio of about 10/1, a pH value between 6·0 and 7·4 (usually on the slightly acid side but rising to alkalinity with age) and is dark or blackish-brown in colour.

The Modified Indore Heap for the Large or Commercial Garden, the Nursery, etc.

In the commercial garden compost heaps must be big in both size and importance. It is a means of supplying edible food to the outside world in exchange for a small proportion of otherwise valueless waste products, provided that costs are saved in its production by efficient and labour-saving methods, and advantages gained in this way are not dissipated by purchase of the most expensive raw materials, or wastage of valuable space. In theory the larger the heap (within reason) the less complicated it is to make, but it needs care in both making and placing, for the commercial gardener's 700-ton Everest in the wrong place, may be in the way of machinery or cover a 6 by 50-foot stretch of crop-producing land for four to nine months, and pay less (in the short-term view) than a crop of early tomatoes. Large heaps should, therefore, be sited off crop-producing land and it

44

should be kept in mind that space is needed for turning both compost and the trailers and machinery which bring in raw materials, tip them directly on to the heap and later cart out the finished product. Usually the smallest vehicle-turning space is required on a central composting site. It is, however, possible to make heaps at several different points on the 5- or 6-acre commercial holding, but such distribution is liable to complicate water supply. Nearness of the large heap to a tap or well, or within reach of a hose, is important, for a ton of straw to be 'composted' by the orthodox method of making 'artificial farmyard manure' needs to be soaked with something like 800 gallons of water, and a large amount is required to moisten even the mixed vegetable matter of the good Indore heap when it is first built. A moderate rainfall provides sometimes, but not always, the moisture required during the composting process, by filtering down through the unroofed surface of the large heap. In a wet area, where very heavy rain is likely to waterlog the heap, or in a very dry area, where hot sun will help to evaporate what little moisture there is in the surface of the heap when it is first made, tree-shelter or other protection is useful. Pumpkins and vegetable marrows are sometimes planted near the base (not on the sides) of the small heap, and trained up over it, to get a similar sun- or rain-sheltering effect.

A site of soil, turf or clay, roughly turned with a cultivator or plough, is better for the large heap than is a foundation of either bricks or concrete. However, the lingering foundation of an old shed or pen (especially if sloped to a sump at one end as are some pig pens), will collect effluent containing about 0·09 per cent of nitrogen, 0·04 per cent phosphates and 0·12 per cent potash (to provide moisture, if necessary, when the heap is turned) and sufficient compost is left behind from one heap to 'inoculate' the next. But there is little point in constructing a special foundation or bin, except for the large heaps of the municipal composting schemes which have to take a great deal of semi-liquid material, such as sewage sludge.

The larger the compost heap (up to a maximum width of 12 feet—it can be of any length), the greater its degree of immunity to weather fluctuations and temperature losses. It maintains its own heat in competition with cool air or wind and against a moderate rainfall; therefore, any enclosure in which it is built is mainly to keep the heap tidy and of good shape and to get it decomposing right to its edges.

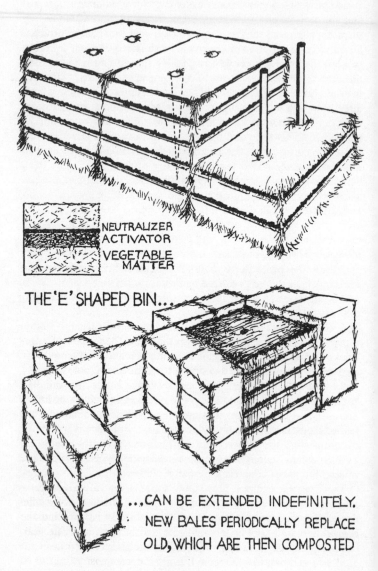

NEUTRALIZER
ACTIVATOR
VEGETABLE
MATTER

THE 'E' SHAPED BIN...

...CAN BE EXTENDED INDEFINITELY. NEW BALES PERIODICALLY REPLACE OLD, WHICH ARE THEN COMPOSTED

Figure 4

COMPOSTING METHODS

For commercial growers, a straw-bale enclosure roofed with corrugated iron is the cheapest. Handling soil in bulk, removing the capping for re-use and even finding sufficient spare soil near the site are all costly in labour. It is cheaper to site the heap where a lorry can drive to it, dump off the bales, and build the heap sides and ends like a letter 'E', with extra compartments, than to handle soil by hand as for the potato clamp, now rapidly being replaced by the storage shed. The bales act first as a perfect heat insulator, and then as further compost material next season when new bales replace old. The straw that is bought should always come in a form that will save labour in handling. Sleepers and uncreosoted timber built into three-sided enclosures are also useful, but more costly.

A large unprotected heap, coated if possible with a thin layer of earth or turves, breaks down well, provided that it is carefuly built and shaped.

The large heap is better completed in separate sections, each of the maximum height, rather than at one time made half the height that it will be eventually and left open for days or weeks to rain and wind. To take a good monthly consignment of waste organic matter, the Battenburg method of heap-placing is a good one to use, because the minimum space is thus required for a composite, continuous heap which permanently chases itself round in circles. The method recommended is, to build the heap in four square sections of the required height (each a separate heap) as and when labour and materials are available; to tack the second section to be built on to the first, the third on to the second, and to close the square with the fourth. By the time this final section is in place (by building at three-weekly to monthly intervals), the first is just about ready for use; its two outer edges (some 6 inches thick) of undecomposed stuff, split off, provide the foundation for the new heap which is built in its place, and the same procedure is used as each section matures in turn. This rotational method works well for the man who gets at one time sufficient material to make only the minimum 5-foot-each-way unprotected heap, perhaps once a month. A different building programme can be used to cope with unlimited wastes, such as the council's tip of roadside cleanings, a good load of straw and the normal harvest of potato, tomato, pea and bean haulm. The heap can be started off with a 10 by 5 foot section (definitely not wider than 12 feet or aeration may be faulty), and other similar sections tacked on to this as soon as more labour is available. Each section matures in turn and the composter's art is in balancing building at one end of the heap with use of the mature compost from the other, so that building is adjusted to available space (the only factor which limits the length of the heap).

The large heap should be built in much the same way as a small heap but there should be a 1-foot foundation of brushwood, thick hedge clippings or any other rough stuff. Hollow air bricks or agricultural drain pipes (spaced 3 or 4 inches apart, endways, in herring-bone fashion the full length and width of the heap) will do as alternatives although they do make things rather awkward when a heap is being turned or carted away. Their use, if no roughage is to hand, involves less chance of disappointment than the results of an airless, too solid heap. Ventilation poles, at the rate of two to every 5- by 10-foot section or one to each 3-foot length of the long heap, should be placed in position beforehand. They are removed as soon as a heap or a section of a large heap has been constructed.

The foundation of rough organic material can be counted as a first layer of vegetable matter, in a heap which will consist of separate layers of this, with other layers of activator and neutralizer between them; otherwise the heap starts with a 6- to 8-inch layer of any available vegetable wastes. The greater the variety the better for this, to provide as varied a diet as possible for fungi and bacteria and to give the richest end-product; also because heaps with a great deal of one vegetable ingredient, often lose to the outside air as gas, or in drainage effluent, much of the plant nutrients which should ultimately go into cultivated soil. Old packing material, straw and hay, the unsaleable or inedible portions of all crops, weeds and anything that can be scrounged or bought in cheaply, can go in. These materials which go to make up the layers of vegetable matter, can be pre-mixed with activator and neutralizer, but this involves extra labour for little return (when compost is being made for ordinary use) as individual wastes can be tipped straight on to the heap to make up the required depth, provided that those close-packing materials, such as sawdust, apple pomace, and coffee grounds, which, if more than an inch thick, impede or prevent air circulation, are added in a light scatter; and fibrous wastes, such as straw, weeds, potato or tomato haulm, are kept below a maximum thickness of 6 inches or so. If much straw or similar low-moisture stuff goes into the vegetable layer, it should be moistened from a fine hose or sluiced from a bucket (by the thatcher's method when wetting straw). Too little rather than too much water should be added; rain coming on to the surface of the unroofed heap will provide much of the moisture required in a temperate climate, where showers are as common as sun's rays for much of the year.

On the first layer of vegetable matter (or the rough foundation) is forked or scattered the organic activator; another 6-inch layer of vegetable matter follows, with neutralizer or base on top of this and then another layer of vegetable matter. In the same layer sequence, this giant double-decker sandwich is repeated to a height of 5 to 6 feet; the heap is then finished off with 2-inch layers of manure and earth or clay, and the ventilation poles wriggled and withdrawn. The heap can rise as high as 7 feet without endangering aeration, provided that it is lightly built and some rough stuff is mixed in to create air spaces, but there is no advantage in going above this highest point that can conveniently be reached with a fork and machinery, and beyond which aeration is almost always poor because of heap compression.

If much fairly fine compost is required quickly, and outside edges of the heap look like hanging fire, a turning can be given at about the end of the first month, when the heap temperature has died down. But to avoid it saves valuable labour, and is preferable to the manhandling which, although more cheaply done with a hand fork than by machinery which can 'eat its head off' by standing idle for long periods, still takes time. There is no point in turning compost in order to put money into the pockets of machinery manufacturers.

A great aid to the quick production of a fine compost which the commercial compost-maker must have for easy packing, transportation and sale in bags and sacks, is to crush or chaff and pre-mix all vegetable ingredients before they go into the heap. The commercial grower, composting for his own use, has not this problem. Unfortunately, apart from some expensive compost turners and mixers (which require several operators) designed mainly for the mushroom grower, and some cutter-blowers, such as the *Robust Universal* or the *Silorator*, designed for the farmer and requiring much more horsepower than the ordinary gardener has available, about the only machine which is both helpful (in producing a fine compost which doesn't need to be turned or sieved) and economical for the ordinary composter, is the old-fashioned chaff-cutter, used as a shredder. Its initial cost is low, but even this is a high price to pay if sieving part of the three-month-old heap is a cheaper method of getting the fine

49

compost required. The owner of a large-type rotary cultivator can, of course, obtain a soil-shredding attachment, mainly designed and used in the preparation of potting soils but capable of breaking up and mixing composting materials. A blade-type rotary cultivator, run several times over tough, resistant stuff, spread on bare ground, will break it up effectively.

The large compost heap, neither turned nor containing chaffed ingredients, is usually ready for ordinary use within three to four months from building in a temperate climate. If it takes longer than this to mature, it is no less valuable: it can be applied to the land at any time, and for this reason, if for no other, compost-making should be a continuous process. Its purpose is the decomposition of organic matter outside the soil, a process carried out by fungi and bacteria which will tackle almost anything of vegetable or animal origin (even odd horses or pigs have gone into some farm heaps), and a great deal else besides, in a heap in which air circulation, moisture content and pH value are controlled by these simple but fairly precise methods. Like the newly-wed's cake that didn't rise, the beginner's first heap or two may be a disappointment, revealed at the end of three or four months as a smelly, black poultice or as effectively preserved as the foliage in a Victorian glass-casket. It takes a little time and trouble to master the art of heap-building for high temperatures at the start of the process in order to get the greatest kill of weed seeds and disease organisms (although the latter, by the complex process of bacterial and fungal antagonisms, are very efficiently dealt with in a 'slow' heap), and for maximum nitrogen fixation and the most efficient release of plant foods. But with perseverance and a little experience, the composter ends up on the right side of the ledger, because the process he exploits is a natural one, and his success can be measured as much by his garden as by his heaps. Some of the difficulties the composter has to face—how to deal with diseased materials, or to get the best potting mixtures without sterilization, for example—are dealt with in other parts of this book. The beginner-composter's main problem is almost always that of finding sufficient organic matter to put into practice a manuring method which can be proved (or disproved by doing it badly) at the minimum of expense and where no vested interest need be allowed to rear its head—in his own garden. His solution is another measure of his success. In many cases a good organic garden with its revenue of weeds and crop wastes, and special green crops, can be entirely self-supporting in organic matter for making compost, the only fertilizer needed.

One very good reason for maximum home-production and saving is that there may be trouble from poison residues on the miscellaneous wastes and industrial by-products brought into the garden from outside. It is not yet known how quickly or completely micro-organisms break down to simpler elements in the compost heap some of the very stable poisons which are used to spray trees and plants. There is little likelihood that they go through the heap entirely unchanged (isolated bacteria are capable of reducing 2,4-D and MCPA to molecular fractions): the danger lies mainly in the encouragement of specialized types of bacteria which might spoil the composting process completely—although they rarely do so, even when washing-up water containing detergent is inadvisedly used to moisten the heap. A well-known brand of disinfectant provides the food supply on which one bacterium flourishes. Breakdown of D.D.T. and other similar substances is probably at the expense of a few generations of 'poisoned' bacteria, too quickly killed and replaced by immune organisms to make any noticeable difference in the composting process. But, until more information is available on this difficult point, the composter uses commercial wastes at his own discretion.

CHAPTER III

ORGANIC MATERIALS:
THEIR USE IN COMPOST AND DIRECT

N
ot the least of the advantages of the compost heap is that it
will take in its stride much industrial refuse that would
otherwise be wasted as well as the ordinary weed and crop-
waste revenue of the garden. There is, however, usually a snag to the
cheapest or 'free-for carriage' wastes, such as the nitrogen-pinching
potential and slow-decay of high-cellulose sawdust, shavings and
spent hops; even the 6 tons of hops to 10 tons of potatoes, or the cart-
load of straw, can become a long-term headache in slow-decaying
organic matter, if badly handled for direct use, or composted without
some other vegetable matter mixed in with them.

In the original recipe for the Indore heap (see *The Waste Products
of Agriculture*, O.U.P.), the late Sir Albert Howard stressed the importance of making compost from as varied a selection of organic
wastes as possible. The result of Howard's experiments when composting single (unmixed) residues (such as green and withered weeds,
cane trash, pigeon-pea stalks, cotton stalks, each with the addition
only of water and combined activator/base in the form of mixed
urine and earth), showed that, often as much as two-thirds longer or
twice the time over the period for conventional composting of a heap
of mixed ingredients is required to yield a usable end-product; that
initial fermentation is in some cases rapid but temperatures often fall
just as rapidly; that loss of as much as 41·8 per cent of nitrogen may
occur from materials rich in this element, and that the heap almost
invariably suffers from faulty (excessive or inadequate) aeration.
These results can be repeated by those composters who want to make
their own mistakes, or who wish to prove that the extra trouble in-
volved in getting a good mixture is well-repaid by freedom from heating, aeration and decomposition troubles. What requires little proof
is that the greater the variety of ingredients in the heap the more likely

are they to provide food for the variety of races of fungi and bacteria which carry out the process of decomposition; and the more varied are the plant foods imported in vegetable matter from deep- as well as shallow-rooted crops and weeds, each with a different chemical and mineral content.

The maximum amount by bulk of a given organic material which can be incorporated as the main part of a heap in which none of the undesirable features of 'solo' recipes are encountered, cannot precisely be established; like every other factor in compost-making, this is variable. In many cases, one individual material, straw for example (when thoroughly wetted), can 'safely' form more than 50 per cent of the vegetable matter in a heap, but what the writer thinks from personal experience is the 'safe' or maximum proportion will be given for most of the farm and industrial waste- or by-products mentioned below.

This chapter, split into alphabetically arranged sections, is mainly written for the man who can get a large bulk of one or two wastes, and the modern specialist producing quantities of one sort of haulm or foliage, who want to know how to use bulk materials safely, because each presents its own problems. It is in no sense intended to by-pass the advice already given: to aim at an 'orchestral' compost; but is designed to help the composter to keep off the rocks, to enable him to expand small quantities of miscellaneous animal and vegetable matter into a great bulk of organic fertilizer, superior even to farmyard manure, by the addition of one or two wastes in bulk, and to give suggestions for direct use of raw organic matter when breakdown outside the soil (composting) gives no distinct advantage or is impossible because of labour shortage. (The object of the first section, a sort of dust cart, is to clear the route of the few unsuitable materials before the procession of useful stuff that can swell the heap as much as the enthusiasm of the composter.)

UNSUITABLE MATERIALS

The composter does not go far wrong if he works on the principle that anything which has once lived can go into his bin or pit; the dead snake, the vase of dusty 'everlasting' flowers turfed out at spring cleaning, even the mildewed haggis and the burst cushion will all help to boost compost production. Most of what is too often prohibited or left out of the heap (often because of its slow decay) by those with little experience, is useful, but there are exceptions.

Rubber, nylon and plastic materials, including rayon, hold the record for greatest resistance to decomposition, and like tin and tinfoil, razor blades, milk bottle tops, and nuts and bolts, should be excluded. Fat, grease and greasy paper in quantity contribute to swill but not to compost, and encourage flies, and at worst mice and rats, if left untidily at the edges of the heap or lying about the composting site. Slow decomposition is the main trouble with bones, from which the fat can be boiled in the kitchen soup pan, but crushing or chopping and treatment in one or two successive heaps can win valuable phosphates from the remains of the Sunday joint.

One bacterium which normally lives by breaking down in urine the phenols which would otherwise accumulate in the soil, swarms when soil is sterilized with carbolic sterilizer and thrives on some disinfectants. Disinfectants and soaps, as they occur strongly diluted with water in septic tanks and cesspools (especially when care is taken to see that not too much of them gets there), also strong caustics, appear to be broken down by the time effluent and sludge arrive at the composting site. But the process of reasserting normal microbiological activity in these valuable activators can be helped by 'weathering' them in a heap of straw, later to be composted. Specialized and not the most useful types of bacteria may also be encouraged in the compost heap by the inclusion of fresh coal ashes and new soot, which contain sulphuretted hydrogen, apart from being over-caustic. Certain minerals, including trace elements, may be lost by putting these tricky materials into the dustbin, but it is the safest way to deal with them, other than by weathering and care, by the methods described in other parts of this chapter.

Inorganic chemicals (and proprietary mixtures of these; always steer clear of the patented product with hush-hush ingredients), are expensively bought as a (normally unnecessary) mineral supplement, or for high nitrogen in an indifferent activator. From the use of sulphate of ammonia and other inorganics to accelerate decomposition in the compost heap, an end-product which is not 'organic', is frequently coarse and may have poor moisture-holding capacity, is obtained often only at the expense of unusual demands for moisture, erratic temperature fluctuations and irregular breakdown. In addition, a single inorganic nitrogen source can lead to specialized bacterial populations, and possibly a microbiologically unbalanced product. Proteins synthesized from inorganic nitrogen, may not be the same as those from protein-containing animal wastes, and the vitamins and growth-promoting substances found in nitrogenous manures are none of them provided by the high-priced concoctions often recommended to the composter.

Good rules are, to keep out of the heap rubber, glass, stones, metals, tins, milk bottle tops, pot cleaners, which will not decay, moth balls and caustic stuff which may kill or deter organisms and to debar anything which encourages specialized populations or mucks up the composting process so far as temperature, aeration and moisture are concerned.

ALLOTMENT RUBBISH

The gradual collection of scarce materials, their storage in a covered bin or pit, for up to a month or five weeks, until a full-sized heap can be made, scrounging, or the growing of special compost crops, are for the individual allotment holder the alternatives to some communal scheme under which wastes from a group of allotments is collected, composted and distributed from a central site by paid or rota labour. This has been tried with success in one or two places; the large heaps which would do credit to the commercial nursery, seem to give courage to chivvy the inevitable shirkers, and for an organized allotment or garden guild, mean little more trouble than that entailed in obtaining concessions, such as the lime subsidy.

On the lone organic garden, an island in a sea of chemicals and sprays, crushing and chopping like firewood (splitting lengthwise and into short lengths), are the best methods of dealing with the inevitable brassica stalks or the occasional parsnip that 'goes down to fly' and, of course, similar contributions from other allotment-holders, to the compost heap and its foundation. Any blighted or slug-ridden potatoes are best crushed, to kill harbouring insects or grubs, for quicker breakdown and to prevent sprouting at the outside of the heap. Faulty carrots and other roots rarely put out secondary growth if first run over with the roller, and disappear quickly even in the small heap; this applies also to the occasional rotten onion, a good earthworm encourager.

The smell from sulphuretted hydrogen in a heap of decomposing cabbage leaves, is almost as bad as that from rotten eggs. This is a measure of the loss to the gardener, which can be avoided if all unwanted brassica foliage is mixed well with lesser quantities of miscellaneous stuff, such as weeds, which for safety should be put into the centre of the heap. As an alternative to straw, potato vines or pea and bean haulms, with any string supports, in bulk help to improve aeration and absorb moisture or, in the heap of dry stuff, break down quickly if well wetted.

The allotment-holder and the town gardener need small bins or pits on a non-spreading site, and the best composting technique possible; their crop-producing area is small and their own supply of organic matter for compost-making is limited. Their main problem can be solved only with ingenuity and skill, or by making the best use of any waste material obtainable to supplement their own residues.

APPLE RESIDUES

Under this heading come commercial 'pulp', 'pomace' or 'mark', the residues from cider-making and other processes, and the inevitable defective fruit which cannot be sold or used for the table.

In the thousand-tree plantation, and often the haphazard domestic 'orchard', composting is the alternative to cleaning up windfalls by means of folded or running pigs or poultry, both of which may mean poor keeping quality of the next crop from over-supply of nitrogen. To compost the rotten and fallen stuff, and fruit small enough to be rejected by the grader, is to avoid the poisonous heap at the end of the orchard which leaves the ground bare, and with a bad smell for a year afterwards, or the needless propagation of many fruit pests.

The rejects in the harvest from the dozen or so trees behind the house and the odd one in the middle of the vegetable bed, are best crushed under a roller on a hard surface to kill grubs, larvae or insects and to prevent the fruit—particularly apples of the hard varieties—from being found still whole when the more readily decayed vegetable wastes have broken down in the heap. This should consist, by bulk, of not more than 30 per cent (preferably less) of the crushed fruit, and about double the normal quantity of ground chalk or limestone (5 per cent by bulk of the vegetable wastes will do), well mixed with partly dry, absorbent material, some rough stuff, such as small tree prunings, and fallen leaves. Such a mixture may give, bacteriologically speaking, a very high-grade analysis, and an end-product particularly suitable for return to the orchard or tree.

In composting large quantities of rejects from the commercial orchard (where crushing would be too costly so composting must be good), at least an equivalent quantity of straw, hedge clippings, bracken, hay or similar stuff, some fresh and green, is needed, with double the usual quantity of neutralizer. For such a mixture a solid activator, such as poultry manure, is better than a liquid one. Although pre-mixing all ingredients helps, it is safe to tip fruit directly on to the large heap, provided that it is placed in thin layers, not more than 3 inches thick, to avoid heat insulation and uneven breakdown. Rain water and fruit juice usually provide necessary moisture for the unroofed heap, and no turning is required unless the end-product is wanted within sixteen to twenty weeks from the date of building. Without turning, whole apples can still be found in the heap after six or seven months. A rough compost is probably the best for a tree mulch, and speedy production is usually unnecessary, as there is merely the necessity to clear the site before the space in the orchard corner is needed for the next season's consignment. The plan and height dimensions of the large heap depend on the materials available, also on the particular trailer combination used to tip the fruit, and some sort of enclosure is needed to hold whole apples which otherwise roll about as fast as marbles on a dance floor. E. M. Bear, in *The Grower*, for 14th June 1952, reported that for a heap 12 feet wide (the maximum width recommended), he used an enclosure made by filling litter between two thicknesses of wire netting, spaced a foot apart and supported by corner posts. Straw bales would be equally effective, assembled into a three-sided rectangular enclosure, with final filling by hand fork or grab over the then closed truck end after the fourth wall had been added.

Commercial 'pulp, 'pomace' or 'mark', obtainable for the cost of collection in some areas, decomposes faster than do crushed apples in the compost heap, but may still take longer than other heap ingredients to break down. Spray treatments which most trees receive tend to make fruit skins tougher and more resistant to decomposition. Much of the poison residue, if any, is removed during essence extraction and other processing but composting is a means of making sure that none gets to the land unchanged. Pulp is not recommended for mulching or direct use because of the danger of poison. There are also other snags; pulp leaves machinery with a very persistent and extremely unpleasant smell and, being a damp and glutinous material, it tends to 'pan' in the heap, unless added to it in thin layers, less than 2 inches thick, or thoroughly mixed and well-aerated with other ingredients; 35 per cent by bulk of the other vegetable wastes in the heap, preferably some green and fibrous stuff, is also about the maximum quantity that can be used with safety for fast composting; at this rate, no watering is necessary unless other materials are very dry. If the pulp is layered in the small heap, it pays to turn at the end of the first month or so. With up to 50 per cent of pulp in the experienced composter's heap (this proportion is not for the beginner, who would probably get, instead of compost, a smelly, sour, jaundiced mass as a result of anaerobic putrefaction), the normal quantity of neutralizer, plenty of dry activator, mixed vegetable matter, no water and no hurry, it is possible to get an end-product with a pH of about 6·1. From a similar mixture (weeds, straw, about 1 per cent by bulk of ground chalk, a herbal activator and pulp, which contains about 1 per cent of potash but less phosphorus) the writer has had good results with strawberries, though yield showed no increase over treatment with compost containing no apple residues. However, as a spring and autumn dressing (a $\frac{1}{2}$ inch thickness in each case) for comparative lawn plots, the same compost tended very effectively to discourage clover-spread over a two-year period.

ASH (Wood ash)

Every good gardener should have a rooted objection to the burning of organic matter, whether diseased or not, which can be rendered into valuable and clean plant foods. The bonfire may be the only place in which to deal with some of the tough, intractable stuff which proves unmanageable to the beginner but too often much valuable organic matter, bacterial and fungal food, and the total of their nitrogen content is needlessly lost to smog- and smoke-laden autumn air during combustion. Altogether ash is a poor return, for the loss of humus-producing material in the form of the woody constituents of leaf skeletons, bark, prunings and rotting seed boxes.

Wood ash, the safest and most valuable variety of ash, supplies only one major plant food in high proportion: potash, which is present at the rate of about 6 per cent in the ash of mixed woods; trace elements and lime (calcium) are recovered from the bonfire, but there is rarely more than 2 per cent of phosphorus. To cash this high potash, and other minerals, wood ash should be used immediately it is produced, or should be stored (sacked, bagged or boxed) well under cover; the equivalent of only 1 to 2 per cent of potash may remain. Wood ash should never be applied directly to the garden soil. F. C. King in *Gardening With Compost* (Faber and Faber) briefly records the case history of a garden soil which was completely ruined in ten years and warns all but the experienced gardener to use wood ash in moderation.

Wood ash contains equal weights of calcium carbonate and potassium carbonate. It is therefore a very efficient neutralizer in the compost heap when used in moderation. To eke out small supplies, it can be mixed with good soil containing free bases or a little old compost. Apart from its neutralizing effect, it contributes potash to compost which is, therefore, especially useful in cases of a deficiency of this element.

If wood is occasionally burnt in the home it is best to keep coal and other fuels off the fire. The ash from coal, coke and smokeless fuels should not be used in the garden at all unless an ash path is being made.

BRACKEN

'There is gold beneath the bracken . . .' is one way of looking at a frond-waving patch which needs little more than a good spring or summer ploughing (with a chain attached to the plough to drag 6 foot foliage and stems into the furrow) to prepare it for bumper potatoes or other potash-lovers. Cultivation and immediate cropping are one of the best methods of controlling this troublesome but valuable weed.

Best value, in terms of potash-rich foliage for mulching or compost-making, is obtained from mid-season bracken, at the first-frond stage, cut in June or July when the potash content may be as high as 2·75 per cent. Later, this valuable element drains down into roots and rhizomes to be stored during the winter, and withered high-cellulose foliage and stems may contain as little as 0·5 per cent potash. Phosphate content is low at all times, about 0·20 per cent, but varies considerably less than does potash and there is 1 to 2 per cent of nitrogen for much of the season.

Green bracken, cut for high potash, nitrogen and moisture (it takes longest to break down if allowed to dry out to high-cellulose), should make up not more than 50 per cent by bulk of the vegetable wastes in the compost heap. It can solve the problem of organic matter shortage only provided that the composter guards against the most frequent troubles in the 'bulk bracken' heap: dryness and heat losses because of open texture. One way to get round these difficulties, is to chaff or chop bracken (the blade-type rotary cultivator can be useful here) and thoroughly wet it before it goes into the heap. A better method is to use it first as litter; it can be a considerable saving on scarce straw and is just about as absorbent when used at the same rate. A good mixture of dung, urine and bracken (plenty from the lower levels in the sty or pen), heaped with ground chalk or limestone, and some additional vegetable matter, watered if necessary, can be made to yield a good rough compost in twelve weeks without turning. The top litter, some of which has dried out before it gets into the heap, takes longer to break down but goes on to the land with no risk of nitrogen robbery. (With about 21 per cent crude protein, the potential feeding value of bracken is tempting, but there is some danger, when animals eat quantities of it over long periods, from poisoning by depletion of the animal body's vitamin 'B' reserves. This in no way affects the use of bracken as litter; the small amounts sorted out and eaten by stock do not cause this trouble.)

One good method of composting fresh bracken (neither chaffed nor as it comes with its own activator in the form of dung and urine in bedding), is to crush and put it in the heap in foot-thick layers, with between them other layers of 3 to 4 inches of farmyard manure, a light sprinkling of earth or old compost, more vegetable matter and a generous helping of ground chalk or limestone (3 to 5 per cent of the total vegetable wastes), in that order. Provided that no ventilation holes are made and each layer of bracken is well-trodden to prevent windy circulation of air, then thoroughly watered to bring it up to the moisture content needed for rapid breakdown, the large well-made heap, earth-covered and once-turned, generates temperatures sufficiently high to kill roots and rhizomes, and the toughest stems are broken down within sixteen to twenty weeks.

The use of 'bracken compost' is one long-term method of correcting potash deficiency, and it can be a valuable safeguard for the monocultural man who loses to the consumer much of this essential element in tubers and fruit from potash-loving tomatoes or potatoes. In the writer's experience, bracken compost is first class for both these crops, as a rooting medium (sieved), for the latter, also for soft fruits and strawberries which seem also to thrive, as do celery and onions, in bracken-mulched soil. One of the advantages of bracken is that it seems unattractive to slugs. Chaffing of bracken to be used as a mulch on cultivated ground, prevents any restriction by brittle or tough stems on hand or machine cultivation; also speeds its breakdown. It can then be used for practically any crop, as witness the Royal Horticultural Society's gardens at Wisley. Cultivated in, it breaks down after several months in the soil; applied in autumn, to the surface of the soil, it is one of the best organic materials the surface cultivator can use to help with the moisture- and heat-retention and soil protection during the winter months.

As a matter of interest, bracken fronds make good packing for vegetables and fruit, particularly apples and cherries. Also, the liquid from fresh, young green fronds, boiled in water, was earlier recommended to be sprayed on rose bushes for aphid control. This bolsters up the writer's courage to mention that once or twice he has observed that bracken compost seems to have a deterrent effect on many aphid species—although this gets us little nearer the reason why!

COFFEE GROUNDS

There is still practically no information for the gardener on the use of spent coffee grounds for mulching or compost-making, even in these days of fabulous profits from by-products. This is a pity, for although there are the inevitable minor snags, grounds are often available free, for the labour of collection and transport, at the rate of the 10 to 12 tons per week turned out by some extractors. Analysis for the commercially-won bulk which can be used at the rate of 15 to 20 per cent of the vegetable matter in the compost heap, or the sink pan consignment which is also useful, is around ·30 per cent phosphoric acid, ·95 per cent potash and 2·69 per cent nitrogen. Even with this high nitrogen, grounds are, unfortunately, useless as an activator; they are slow-decaying and dry out quickly.

In the small compost heap, grounds should be thoroughly mixed with other ingredients and a little more chalk or limestone than usual; in the large heap, layers should be added (if pre-mixing is impossible) not more than $1\frac{1}{2}$ inches thick, or air circulation may be prevented by 'blanketing'. For the expert composter, a heap consisting of one part of coffee grounds to four of lawn mowings and two of straw or other clean, rough material, by bulk, with a good sprinkling of ground chalk or limestone, plus fine earth or old compost mixed in before the heap is lightly built on a good thick, open heap foundation, gives a fine friable compost, free of weed seeds, in fifteen to twenty weeks. Such a heap does not need to be turned or watered, until the end of the first month, and very little activator is required, in the experience of the writer. Earthworms are specially attracted to this mixture, apparently by the grounds which are a recommended food for their culture by 'worm farming' methods.

Any large bulk of grounds that cannot be put into the compost heap, can be stacked in the open without serious loss. Left in a low heap for two or three years, for breakdown by bacteria, fungi and, particularly, earthworms, they give a finely divided rotted product, especially useful for improving heavy clay when dug in at the rate of about half a bucketful to the square yard in the autumn. Culti-vated under at times other than this, the raw grounds are liable to cause nitrogen starvation, of course. Rotted grounds can be used as a mulch, not more than 1 to $1\frac{1}{2}$ inches deep, for practically all crops; raw, they take longer to break down than when rotted, but are better than lawn mowings for moisture retention and more efficient for control of annual and the less hardy perennial weeds.

FEATHERS AND FEATHER WASTES

Apart from the few choice specimens which end up on ladies' heads or hats, and those which go to hop gardens (to be cultivated in at the rate of 1 ton or more per acre), our poultry farms' vast output of feathers is normally sent up in smoke. Thus is lost to the land valuable organic matter, and a useful 7 to 10 per cent of nitrogen (though but little potash and phosphorus) which could easily be trapped by the poultry farmer or the gardener living near him: by means of the compost heap.

Composting of feathers, rather than their direct use, rules out the danger of disease risk to birds, an important consideration for the backyard poultry-keeper; it also speeds the breakdown of the tough skeletons of large wing- and tail-feathers, which otherwise decay but slowly in the soil, cause a nuisance during ordinary hoeing by hand or machine, and look unsightly while sticking, like porcupine quills, out of vegetable beds or flower borders. A few shafts normally re-main in the unturned compost heap at the end of a three-month com-posting period, but subsequently break down well in soil, moist and biologically rich because well-composted. Feathers, because dry and tough, need to be moistened into the ordinary Indore heap, which should contain about three times their quantity of fresh, green veget-able matter with plenty of heating power. Russian Comfrey foliage (any excess over fodder requirements) is first class with feathers, when both are mixed with some poultry manure, the activator most likely to be available in quantity.

Entirely unused as a fertilizer in the ordinary way are the 'insides' and bits of skin from table birds dressed for market by the poultry farmer. To enable the poultry farmer or gardener to handle this somewhat obnoxious material safely, a special composting method is recommended in Chapter IV.

GRASS, LAWN MOWINGS AND STREET CLEANINGS

In Pepys's day the spilt chaff and horse dung from Fleet Street would have been wizard for the Indore composter, had he existed. Now, the mixture of asphalt, grit, weed seeds, paper, cigarette and ice-cream cartons (with the exception, in the autumn, of leaves which are well worth the trouble of collection even with the slight tar danger), the usual revenue from country and town road-sweeping everywhere, is fit for little other than salvage, and not always that. Roadside grass clippings are useful, however; and particularly valuable to the town composter, are the mowings which, on municipal gardens and lawns, usually end up on the bonfire. The public's loss in terms of diminished soil fertility (because valuable organic matter goes up in smoke), even in terms of ever-increasing rates (to which the high cost of 'artificials' to replace lost plant foods, may be a contribution on a 'drop-in-the-ocean' basis), can be the gardener's gain. Lawn mowings lack fibre and need careful handling, but can contribute to the recovery of a town garden, starved of organic matter, as quickly and for much less cost than that of expensive organic manures.

At least every other time the garden lawn is cut, the mower-box should be left off the machine, to allow grass clippings to return their own weight in moisture and manurial value to one of the most unnatural parts of the garden. Any surplus of mowings over ordinary composting requirements from alternate cuttings, can be treated in a special heap, or used in a variety of ways other than this, all a vast improvement on the production of a useless green, slimey rice pudding, created by airlessness, moisture and acidity, in the pile out of sight behind the summer-house or the parked garden roller.

The necessity in a special composting method is, to use a quantity equal in bulk to available lawn mowings of dry, fibrous material, such as straw, dry spent hops, even peat, and to mix these together thoroughly. Without a good deal of added fibre, the amount of 'compost' you get from the heap consisting mainly of lawn mowings is small, and without rough stuff to create air spaces, mowings compact into an airless putrefying mess. Despite these difficulties, you can get a fine end-product, free of weed seeds, if the mixture is good and other stuff that goes into the heap is clean. You can get within three months just the sort of compost that is first class for seed and potting work, without turning or sieving, from a good heap which consists of: equal parts of mowings, straw or chopped green bracken, less than the normal quantity of activator (less because of the readily decayed proteins and carbohydrates in the grass), up to 3 or 4 per cent of ground chalk or limestone (a little more than usual), all left unwatered unless a need for moisture is apparent after the first month.

In *Compost Making, The Quick Return Method*, p. 12 (Intensive Gardening Press), Miss Maye E. Bruce recommends a fast method for handling mowings in bulk, and gives a recipe: three parts of mowings to one of dry fibre in dry hops or *old* leaves, the mixture to be heaped lightly in a bin and treated with the Q.R. herbal activator (see Appendix I). It is claimed by the originator that compost can be made in fourteen days by this method.

Any large quantity of lawn mowings such as can sometimes be got from the council's tipping, is best put into a special compost heap (a quarter by bulk of farmyard manure and some ground chalk or limestone) well watered, and given time fully to break down and exhibit its crop of seedling docks and thistles, if it has not heated well.

GREENGROCERS' WASTES

The usual consignment of greengrocers' waste is a mixture of stuffs, some of which (often by the crateful) gave up the ghost long before it was to have become pawn in the game of selling to housewives with no scope or capacity for selective buying. Gangrenous oranges, shrivelled aubergines, squashed tomatoes and bananas, dropsical marrows, and the outside leaves of vegetables with straw, shavings, wood, cardboard and 'non-returnables', make an excellent compost, provided the high-moisture snag is kept in mind. The mixture in the heap must consist of at least a third by bulk of dry, fibrous stuff to go with the green material of high-moisture content, and so eliminate all danger of putrefaction. Wood shavings, straw or even sawdust are excellent and contribute to a fine, weed-free end-product, when mixed with double or treble the quantity of greengrocers' mixed wastes, plus 5 to 6 per cent of ground chalk or limestone, by bulk of this mixture, and a little earth (if this is not added on roots) or old compost, lightly heaped, well ventilated, but left unwatered. The mixture may still be wet at the end of the first ten to twelve days and, if so, a turning given then will help to disperse excess moisture without seriously affecting the heating-up process. If putrefaction occurs because of over-wetness of the first heap, the only cure is to remake it, and to add more dry material and activator. Sixteen weeks in the well-made small heap, often much less in a larger, is sufficient to yield a high quality end-product from good, mixed wastes.

HAIR AND HAIR WASTE

Hair has previously gone unmentioned by most compost writers, despite the fact that its use in compost-making is just the sort of odd idea that has sales value for Sunday newspapers. But it has not gone unused by practical organic gardeners, few of whom ignore any possible source of humus-forming material, especially 'free-for-carriage' wastes, odd-seeming or not.

Hair, often goat hair (by the 4 cwt. bale, if long, or loose if it is short stuff mixed with straw, chaff and dirt), which can sometimes be obtained from abattoirs, tanneries, or government wool-disinfecting stations, has almost always been formaldehyde-treated. Composting it is therefore recommended: to get rid of the chemical residue without damage to the soil population, also because hair otherwise decays to release its 10 per cent of nitrogen very slowly into the soil, meanwhile causing a nuisance during ordinary cultivations though its texture-improving quality is useful, particularly on heavy clay. Similar treatment is advised of the barber's bounty of short human hair, which usually is well-seasoned with brilliantine and talcum powder—not an ideal diet supplement for fungi and bacteria. Large quantities of hair, short or long, break down well in the ordinary Indore heap if well moistened, then mixed or interlayered with plenty of fresh, green vegetable matter.

HEDGE CLIPPINGS

The fine clippings which come from immaculate hedges and trees that have been kept short by topiary work, not allowed to grow too long for appearance or the shears, break down quickly in the conventional compost heap. Larger clippings and fruit tree prunings are mentioned here because they are just the thing for the foundation of a large heap, if layered a foot or so thick before the compost heap is built up. The fungal decay of dead wood does not matter beneath the heap, and the foundation can later be composted to bring into circulation the relatively stable and resistant lignin and woody matter which few of our short-lived crop plants have time to form in any quantity. Use all the small and medium-sized clippings and prunings you can get, under or in the heap, and put the large ones on the bonfire.

HOP WASTES

High-grade spent hops are added to animal feeding stuffs to supply protein and carbohydrate. Horticultural suppliers cash in on less good samples, which analyse at about 0·02 per cent potash, 0·14 per cent phosphate and 0·65 per cent nitrogen, by fortifying them with organic (for high-class horticultural work) and inorganic (and less expensive) supplements, and selling them as 'balanced manures'. For the compost gardener, who is concerned as much with organic matter as with chemical analysis, spent hops, direct from the brewery, represent equal value for less cost, and provide useful bulk for composting or direct use.

Spent hops, mulched or cultivated in at 10 to 15 tons to the acre (over half a bucketful to the square yard) in the autumn, preferably after rain, or previously well-wetted rather than applied in the semi-dry state in which they are bought, decompose rapidly in the top 2 to 4 inches of soil. But because their nitrogen content is low, the quantity of this element in something like a ton of poultry manure or its equivalent (to each 10 tons of hops), should go in with them to prevent nitrogen starvation and speed breakdown if a dressing is to be followed by immediate cropping, as it is sometimes in greenhouses. With autumn application of hops and normal spring cropping, the nitrogen supplement is unnecessary. Alternatively, spent hops can be stored in an untreated heap over the winter, to provide a fine semi-decayed product which can be cultivated in in early spring, three to four weeks before sowing, also without the nitrogen-robbery risk. The non-digger, of course, can apply the raw stuff at any time: as a mulch, 3 to 4 inches thick in the autumn, between crop rows during spring and summer (mainly for moisture retention), and in maximum quantity to maintain a foot-thickness of organic matter out to the drip-line of any variety of fruit tree, but particularly the thirsty plum. A thin surface dressing of spent hops, kept wet by moisture absorbed during watering and from the underlying soil, has been found to encourage fungus troubles in tomatoes, under orthodox greenhouse management. However, the same crop in similar conditions, has done well under a thick surface mulch (spent hops at the rate of 15 tons per acre of bed), the surface of which dries out quickly after watering.

On light soils, and less so on others, the effect of spent hops is similar to that of straw, but, in the writer's opinion, best value is obtained via the compost heap. A recipe which has been found useful, is: equal amounts by bulk of spent hops and vegetable wastes, a very small quantity of sawdust or shavings, a little less of the activator than is usual (unless there is much woody matter) because nitrogen is quickly released from the hops, and 1 to 2 per cent of ground chalk or limestone—all mixed well together. The hops, if dry, need to be thoroughly moistened before the heap is made and with, where possible, rough materials as a base beneath the heap. A ventilation hole will be necessary if the heap is a large one. The mixture should be watered again if it dries out by evaporation, as it often does, after ten to fourteen days, when watering and turning can be given in one operation, if a really fine product is required in the shortest space of time.

On practically all hop gardens, bines containing up to 0·28 per cent nitrogen and 0·9 to 1·0 per cent of both potash and phosphorus (not counting the nutrients in readily decomposable string which can go into the compost heap with them), are burnt, since feeding them to stock has generally been abandoned because of danger from poison residues. A composting method for them is recommended here: more for gardeners, such as one of the writer's friends living in Kent, who can save from the bonfire and take from a local hop garden, any quantity of bines he requires, than for hop growers themselves. (As a matter of interest, however, the late Sir Albert Howard, in *Farming and Gardening for Health or Disease* (Faber), mentions that on a well-known hop garden, the cost of producing and applying 10,000 tons of finished 'humus' (compost) a year, made from pulverized town wastes (transported in from a considerable distance), hop bines and string, and local animal and vegetable wastes, was less than would have been required to purchase and apply an equivalent dressing of

ORGANIC MATERIALS

'artificials'.) Not more than three-quarters of the vegetable wastes in the heap should consist of hop bines and string, cut roughly into short lengths for the small bin or pit. They can go on to the heap in layers, a foot thick and thoroughly watered, with between them, other layers of activator (if farmyard manure, a quarter by bulk of the total vegetable wastes), and sprinklings of ground chalk or lime-stone. A little compression with the feet does no harm as soon as the heap is built. Extra watering is often necessary when the small pile is turned at the end of the first month, but rain water usually provides sufficient moisture for the large, unprotected heap. Four to five months is long enough for the composting process, if no turning is given.

KITCHEN AND DOMESTIC WASTES

To make the compost heap the dustbin of the country house, where the dustman never calls and no pigs or chickens are kept to clean up edible stuff, can solve problems in garbage disposal as well as reap dividends in improved crops and soil. The contents of the sink pan and the vacuum cleaner, and much of the haul from the annual spring cleaning, come into the same category as salad dressing for the mixed vegetable wastes, roadside grass and other foliage, which can be collected for the compost bin in any country district.

Tea leaves and spent coffee grounds are both caviare to earth-worms and, in the quantity that comes daily from the kitchen, can be scattered straight on to the compost heap. Not all organic gardeners will eat potatoes cooked with their jackets on, despite advantages in flavour and 'roughage' at the cost of a little unsightliness when mashed; peelings from these, from onions, parsnips and all vegetables break down quickly in the centre of the heap and rarely, if ever, sprout. The ash of banana, apple and lemon skins, respectively, contains approximately 41 per cent, 26 per cent and 31 per cent of potash, which can be cashed without burning, despite the toughness which makes the peelings of much-sprayed fruit slow to break down and less attractive to worms than they should be. Eggshells and the clinker from the bottom of the kitchen kettle cannot be relied on as a 'base' in the heap, because their lime is in a locked-up form, but they break down slowly after crushing, or go through the heap to complete decomposition in the soil without hazard to machinery or cultivation. The snag attached to waste scraps of meat or fish, which

68

supply readily decayed material and substances not present in green foliage, is that they attract flies, or at worst, rats and cats. Unless they can be put well inside the compost heap or be stored under a pile of earth, where they break down without smell almost as quickly as they go bad during a summer heatwave, these should be burned or put in the dustbin. Fat and grease should be kept out of the heap; bones can usefully go in, if first boiled or put through the soup pan (to remove fat and grease which would otherwise act as preservatives to already tough cartilage), then chopped into small pieces or crushed on a hard floor. If placed in a remembered part of the heap, large pieces of bone which have failed to break down by the time the heap is in other respects ready for use, can easily be transferred to a further heap.

Woollen carpet sweepings contain equivalent slowly available nitrogen to that in nitrate of soda and in small quantities can go into the heap along with the contents of the ashcan, the tattered and smelly dishcloth, string, small bits of rag (not oily) and old scraps of material, other than plastic or nylon, provided that plenty of fresh green stuff is mixed in with them. Only in quantity and because of dryness do they slow down the composting process completely. For this reason, discarded clothing, from old socks to overcoats, should be torn into small pieces, well-wetted, and added bit by bit to successive heaps. Only buttons and buckles remain after several weeks. Old boots and shoes do not disintegrate well and are best omitted from small heaps.

LEATHER WASTE ('DUST')

The leather industries' finely pulverized wastes and soft leather scraps go unused by most gardeners, although small quantities are sometimes cultivated in for pricked-out brassicas and for plums on heavy clay. Leather contains a useful quantity of nitrogen and minerals, but decays slowly in the soil; composting, which speeds decay, is recommended to the organic gardener, who can usefully add a good quantity of fine leather or leather waste, first moistened, to the ordinary Indore heap which contains plenty of fresh vegetable wastes.

LEAVES AND LEAF-MOULD

Leaves quickly rot during winter or are dragged down into fertile soil by earthworms. If left where they fall, or mulched on open, cultivated ground, to form the nearest we can get to nature's forest floor with its soil-protective and weed-strangling effects, few remain on the soil surface until late spring, unless a high wind has sent them careering off into a drift in the angle of the garden wall. One solution to this main problem of 'blowing' when leaves are mulched (as they can be for all vegetable crops and many flowers, especially those in the herbaceous border), is to add on top of them a light sprinkling of earth, old compost, or, better still, ground chalk or limestone, which at 2 oz. to the square yard will also deal with otherwise mounting acidity where oak leaves, and some others, are used in quantity. Yew leaves, which are extremely poisonous, should not be mulched where they are liable to be picked up by grazing stock. For a little extra trouble, the production of good leaf-mould rules out the blowing menace, and reaps dividends in that it costs less to produce than does peat to buy. It is a good substitute for peat or superior to it, as one ingredient of potting mixtures, for ordinary indoor bulbs as well as most greenhouse plants. Its use is, also, often the only way to feed up a town garden, starved of organic matter and so small that the production of good compost is difficult, if not impossible. The amount of compost you can make depends on the variety as well as the quantity of organic matter you can get, the amount of leaf-mould merely on the quantity of leaves. Even the town gardener can obtain a great bulk of these every autumn. He has, of course, to be 'quick on the draw' to trap the minerals and trace elements brought up from beneath the pavements by the foraging roots and great circulatory systems of trees; autumn leaves are embarrassing to the authorities and are often too soon whisked away in the corporation cart, the Black Maria of town horticulture, before a tip to the street cleaner can land them over the garden fence.

When making leaf-mould, the only equipment required is a length of wire netting and four corner posts, to make an enclosure not less than 2½ feet square, the purpose of which is to prevent blowing and keep the heap tidy (not heat insulation or weather-protection). The bigger the heap the better, but as no other ingredients are used, its size depends on the quantity of leaves available. The best leaves to use are beech and oak; the worst, evergreens and plane leaves with their woody, Methuselah skeletons. The method of building is to place in position a foot layer of leaves, to tread and thoroughly water this, to add more leaves, tread and water again, layer upon layer until the bin is packed solid. The job is then finished. No protection is needed on either the top or sides of the heap, for rain which gets well in and down will do no harm and will prevent purely fungal decay (similar to 'fire-fang' of stable manure) at the bottom; no other vegetable matter should be allowed to bring in weed seeds (which would not be killed in the absence of the high temperatures such as are achieved during compost-making); no neutralizer or activator is needed, as the aim is slow decay into a sort of 'vegetable cheese', valuable as a moisture-retaining sponge and source of slowly available plant foods.

Like good wine, leaf-mould improves with age. One year's decay gives from the heap a product which is still liable to 'blow' and may contain viable weed seeds, two years or more the increasingly valu-able solid mass like plug tobacco which is as good as horticultural peat in almost all cases, and distinctly better in Alpine potting mixtures. Five, even ten years is not too long to wait for the finest variety of leaf-mould from the first of a hierarchy of heaps, built year after year with leaf-fall regularity. Unfortunately, the town gardener usually needs to mulch or cultivate it in by the end of the second or third autumn, but at least a part of each heap should be left for later use. This mature leaf-mould, which is richer in plant foods than peat and has all its advantages, is then best used for greenhouse or indoor work, as an ingredient of potting mixtures, for which it should be teased through a $\frac{1}{2}$-inch mesh (smaller for seeds), the sievings put into the bottom of trays and boxes, for drainage.

Much of their 'vitality' has been lost by the time leaves fall. This is no disadvantage when they are used to make leaf-mould, but their little nitrogen, waterproof covering, resistant skeletons and propensity to 'pack' as slickly as playing cards and exclude air from the heap, make bulk composting difficult unless leaves are thoroughly mixed with a rich activator, such as poultry manure, and about treble the quantity (by bulk, compared to leaves) of fresh, green vegetable matter. This is never available when it is most wanted: in the autumn, so that the quantity of leaves which can be composted then is limited. Only a very few leaves go without trouble into the October heap which consists, more often than not, mainly of exhausted, high-cellulose foliage and stems from the herbaceous border. One way to get round this difficulty is to prepare leaves for spring composting: to stack both deciduous and evergreen leaves (not pine needles, which are particularly useful as a mulch for strawberries, or plane leaves which are best left in a 'dunce's' heap for several years) in the autumn, as for making leaf-mould, but lighter and with 2 to 3 per cent of ground chalk or limestone and about a quarter by bulk of farmyard manure (or alternative activator) added. The somewhat quicker breakdown obtained by this method than when making leaf-mould, enables a semi-rotted material, not unlike rough peat, to be mixed in with about double the quantity of fresh green vegetable matter, neutralizer and activator as usual, in the spring compost heap. If necessary, this bastard leaf-mould can be used by the surface cultivator for spring mulching, but it should not be cultivated in or used for potting mixtures because there is still some danger of nitrogen starvation. Only the finest leaf-mould, carefully made, is as 'safe' as peat in all respects.

MALT DUST ('CULMS')

This brewery residue (barley rootlets and shoots which sprout during the malting process, are then shrivelled by heat and finally removed by screening) is valuable to the gardener because of its readily decayed organic matter, which contains roughly 3 per cent of nitrogen, 1·5 per cent phosphorus and 2 per cent potash. Because its moisture content is rarely higher than 10 per cent, it should be thoroughly moistened when it goes into the Indore heap, or be cultivated in after rain if used direct on vegetable and flower borders.

PEAT

Horticultural moss or sedge peats are sterile and weed and disease free. They are chemically neutral or acid but not below pH 3·5. Peat should never be added to the compost heap. This organic material is low in plant foods but is useful as a soil conditioner and as a mulch. Peat is expensive and the amounts used in the garden are not liable to lead to an acidic soil condition.

RABBIT WASTES

Rabbits' feet, ears and tails are sometimes obtainable at little cost from fur trimmers or dealers in the skin trade, also from dealers who handle the small quantities imported. These wastes contain approximately 10 per cent of nitrogen, plus some phosphorus, can usefully be added to the ordinary compost heap, managed by the method recommended in Chapter IV.

ORGANIC MATERIALS

SAWDUST, CHIPWOOD AND SHAVINGS

There used to be lashings of this stuff around but nowadays it is only the gardener living near a sawmill or a similar factory who may be able to obtain some. This organic waste product is only half as rich in the major plant nutrients as corn straw, with only 4 lb. of nitrogen, 2 lb. of phosphorus and 4 lb. of potash locked up in a ton. These by-products of the timber industry need careful treatment by the gardener. As little as 3 tons of sawdust cultivated into an acre of highly fertile soil will cause nitrogen starvation of most crops except peas and beans. Sawdust, chipwood and shavings have a bad reputation in horti-culture because of their carbon/nitrogen ratio of roughly 250/1. There is an extremely slow breakdown of pentosans, cellulose and lignin with some toxicity from turpenes, resins, tannins and sulphides released during the decay of some woods, mostly evergreens. In spite of these snags, organic gardeners have shown how sawdust, both soft and hardwood, can be handled to great advantage with the minimum of danger and effort.

The first rule is never to use sawdust on a poor soil. Fertility must first be built up by means of generous applications of good, ordinary compost, in order to encourage the enormous bacterial and fungal population required for the breakdown of this most resistant form of organic matter. Sawdust should then be used sparingly *on* (not in) the soil and, until experience has been gained, only after its prelimin-ary 'weathering'. This 'weathering' is essential when the beginner first handles sawdust, and advisable for the experienced composter who digs; it is unnecessary only for the organic surface cultivator (see Appendix II) who puts it as a thin 'icing' on the top of a heavy autumn mulch of ordinary compost and never lets it get into the soil until the second year, a winter having intervened.

'Weathering', in other words advancing decomposition outside the soil or the compost heap, reduces the excess carbon in sawdust which makes it safer for direct use, and brings the time needed to compost it nearer that required for the breakdown of less resistant wastes. It takes time, but need not take up valuable crop-producing space, or mean much extra work, if sawdust is spread: up to 3 to 4 inches thick, where it will soak up excess moisture round the composting site, on fallow ground to act as a weed control, or thinly on the garden path for the same purposes and to give a good, clean working surface in the worst weather. Within a few months, under the combined action of rain, sun, wind, invading fungi, bacteria and earthworms, its pale ochre colour when fresh, turns to the light, boot-polish brown that is the equivalent of the 'amber' traffic light, the go-ahead signal to prepare for composting or mulching.

The writer finds it necessary to leave a 4-inch layer of sawdust or chipwood for nine months or so in a London garden, but more sure safeguards than a set time limit for 'weathering' are: over-wintering, brownness throughout and earthworms treating sawdust like ordinary soil. The newness wearing off is not enough as only the outside crust of a large heap becomes brown, like the skin of a rice pudding, after several months—the reason for spreading sawdust thinly on a 'thinner the layer, the slicker the decomposition' principle. Softwood sawdust takes *longer* than does the hardwood variety to decompose.

Weathered sawdust, chipwood or shavings should *not* first be used direct on flower- and vegetable-beds on the organic garden, whether surface cultivated or not. It should be introduced via the compost heap. Not more than 5 to 8 per cent of sawdust, by bulk of other vegetable wastes, should go into the first few heaps. This allows the composter to become accustomed to this slow-decaying ingredient and the soil to a new item of diet when the end-product is applied after a slightly longer composting period than is usual. For the first year, the resultant compost should be used for peas or beans, or if absolutely necessary, for other leguminous crops which, like these, are self-sufficient in nitrogen. In general it should not be applied where non-legumes are to be grown, until the soil has received at least one application of such special compost when down to legumes. It is impossible for the ordinary gardener to know whether the carbon/nitrogen ratio in the 'sawdust' compost is the same as that of the soil to which it is to be applied, and trouble may result if it is not. The obvious safeguard is to apply the compost to peas and beans which are moved round the garden in rotation, then, and only then, to use it elsewhere for other crops.

During the second and third years, the proportion of sawdust which is put into each heap can be increased. By the fifth and sixth years, the skilled non-digging composter can safely use equal quantities of fresh, green vegetable matter and sawdust, the latter wetted if not thoroughly moist from 'weathering'. The composting method is of some importance. Sawdust or other wood wastes, used in bulk, must be thoroughly mixed with other ingredients, as layers more than

74

$\frac{1}{2}$ inch thick will 'pan' and prevent air circulation throughout the heap. Allowance must also be made for very low nitrogen by using half as much again of one of the dung-type activators. Poultry manure is the best, as it is extra-strong and also favours the most powerful bacteria capable of breaking down woody and fibrous organic matter. Alternatively, sawdust can first be used as litter and thereby be enabled to satisfy its own excessive nitrogen requirements. Fine varieties of sawdust absorb more urine than do either chipwood or shavings, but all can solve the major litter problem of the riding stable and the backyard poultry run. Wood waste may be too cold for pigs, but cows seem to prefer this to corn straw for bedding, and as it is not dusty it is considerably more hygienic round the dairy. Young leguminous growth, from annual lupins, and Russian Comfrey foliage is a good 'accelerator' of sawdust, which also breaks down well when mixed with sea and water weeds, which themselves are prevented from slipping in the stack. A mixture of sawdust and a little wetted straw, with lawn mowings (which contribute readily decayed ingredients of good heating power in exchange for fibre and aeration) makes for a finely divided, weed-free end-product. Mixtures, such as wood waste with dry bracken, peat, much straw, or high-cellulose autumn foliage, should be avoided, as these latter materials have no heating power and are poor in nitrogen. A little more than the normal amount of ground chalk or limestone should go into the heap, and fish heads or ground rock phosphate can be added if a phosphate balancer, to compensate for the scarcity of this element in sawdust, is considered advisable. All ingredients should be mixed together thoroughly, the heap should be carefully built, well-aerated, turned twice and moistened if necessary at the end of the first and second months after building, and left for at least two to three months longer than usual to mature.

Wood waste compost is normally ready for use six to seven months from the date of building the heap. For the first year on soil which has previously received compost containing very small quantities of sawdust, it should be applied at the rate of not more than 10 tons to the acre, preferably as an autumn mulch, again to the plot where peas and beans are to be planted, until the whole garden has been treated with this more 'concentrated' compost. It is, however, better gradually to increase the quantity of sawdust used, rather than to jump from a small proportion to a large one in successive heaps, so that the end-product can then be applied at increasing yearly rates of application, to practically any part of the garden. On the writer's vegetable plots, it has given good results with all crops except raspberries. It has been found particularly good for both light and heavy soils, for moisture retention and drainage; has been used extensively to supplement ley mowings as a mulch for all fruit trees; and, at the rate of 15 to 20 tons to the acre, for gooseberries and strawberries, *always as a surface dressing on fertile soil*. It should not be used in potting mixtures until safety to do so is demonstrated by success with trial pots of greenhouse plants. It should not be cultivated in for several months after application, the best time for which is autumn as this allows any undecomposed fragments (particularly of shavings or chipwood) to break down during the winter, on the soil surface. Much the same applies to the direct use of 'weathered' sawdust.

For the cultivator, the complications of mulching with sawdust, chipwood or shavings may outweigh advantages. There is a necessity for quick changes of annual crops which often have to go where there is available space, not always in rotation, and peas and beans are the only crops which survive on the strength of their own nitrogen supply. The ordinary organic cultivator, whose method of cultivation (soil disturbance) is not very different from the orthodox man's, only shallower, is not advised to dig in uncomposted sawdust, or to use it as a mulch, unless he applies it in a *very* light scatter (not more than enough to cover the surface) directly after weed clearance and ground tidying in the autumn. Apart from composting, to limit the quantity used is the only safeguard against having to turn in much nitrogen-ravenous, half-raw stuff when making a seed-bed in the following spring.

The surface cultivator, however, is perfectly safe in trying sawdust first 'weathered' and later 'raw', as a mulch on fertile soil, which has previously been composted in the ordinary way. For the first year on undug soil, the 'weathered' variety should be spread, not more than ½ inch thick, at no greater rate than about 9 tons to the acre (on the patch where peas and beans are to go in the following spring). It should be placed on top of the normal, autumn compost mulch, immediately after this is applied, to allow the greatest time to elapse between application and possible soil disturbance when planting out or harvesting crops. As the soil becomes used to the new material, applied always to the legume part of the rotation until the whole garden has been covered, greater quantities of raw sawdust, chipwood or shavings can be applied (with 1 cwt. of ground chalk or limestone to each ton of sawdust), for all but the acid-lovers, and a ground rock phosphate balancer, if this is thought necessary. No maximum quantity which can be used for all surface-cultivated crops (except raspberries, which, in the writer's experience, should receive none) can be fixed. The only snag when mulching with raw sawdust on the undug garden is that it sometimes attracts frost, even under cloches, where ordinary compost (with or without sawdust) appears to be much safer on this score. However, a simple safeguard against this, is to go over the garden with a hose, in early spring, to make sure the sawdust remains wet.

The main insurances against trouble, above or below ground on which wood waste of any sort is used, are, to keep this material in sight on the surface until it is indistinguishable from ordinary soil, or to put it through the compost heap, and in either case to wean both garden and crops to this cheapest of all industrial wastes.

The cheapest material of all is the small shavings, plus a little sawdust, from mechanical planing machines. Sawdust has some market and it is therefore often charged at so much a bag, but the planing-machine waste is usually free for cartage. This is best used in the orthodox deep-litter house, where its excess-cellulose heat is spent in warming up the poultry. After six months it is reduced to a brown powder which can be used on the farm as a direct top dressing for pasture, or stacked as a kind of low-grade activator with an equal bulk of green material, or on its own. For safety it still has some rotting to do, so treat it as compost which has had its first turn, stack with crowbar air holes, like a normal heap, and let it rot for a further three months or more; or use it on the surface direct. Well-managed deep-litter is half-made compost, and the finest way of converting shavings to fertility-building that there is, for the fierce nitrogen of the poultry dung has used itself up by cracking the cellulose.

SEAWEED

Mechanically processed and fortified seaweed, in the form of a bagged or bottled fertilizer or feeding stuff, promises to be as familiar to the Warwickshire gardener who has never seen the sea, as are the custard powder and soups and sauces in which he doesn't recognize its alginic acid, or derivates of it, used as thickeners. Unfortunately, it may be that valuable organic matter is lost during the canning of minerals, trace elements and other substances, in the processing of

8 to 10 tons of seaweed down to 1 ton of powder, by reducing it to a fine grist and rotary drying it for three-quarters of an hour at a temperature much higher than that in an electric sterilizer. However, it is still the only method of getting this valuable fertilizer to the soot- and rain-soaked midland garden. Even the high speeds (and higher costs) of modern transport barely get harvested seaweed, with sand, and over 80 per cent water much beyond the range of sea fogs, beneficial or otherwise, before it yields its marine corpses to fly maggots and exchanges the smell of the sea for that of the sewer. The value of seaweed fertilizer, like that of many other liquid or powdered organics, mainly lies where the real thing cannot be obtained; in this case, inland. Near the coast, the seaweed that recently caused more trouble and got more headlines than the 'bikini', because of the beach fly menace, wins hands down in the writer's opinion, if it can be collected behind the 'combine harvesters' of storms and tides without putting the price sky high in labour terms. Collection is a messy and expensive operation, and one definitely not for the female but, where it is possible, unlimited quantities of easily managed organic matter, with few snags, can solve the coastal gardener's main problem: that of obtaining sufficient 'binding' and humus-forming material for easily blown and readily leached soils.

For top value, seaweed is best harvested in later summer, autumn or after winter storms, as battering has an effect on analysis, but at any time a good mixture of weeds is rich in the variety of minerals and other substances every gardener or stock-keeper values. From *Pelvetia canaliculata* at high-water mark, down to *Laminaria digitata* at low, and *L. cloustoni* out of reach of all but the scoops and grappling hooks of marine culture machinery, mixed seaweeds are the richest source of all the known trace elements, although no species contains every one. These minerals and 4 to 15 per cent of protein, high carbohydrate and a vitamin content the same as that of green vegetables, make the brown weeds a valuable supplementary feed for cows, sheep, pigs, ducks and poultry (when made available, but not forced on them in some hypothetically correct proportion in bulk stock feed; they should be allowed to choose what they want).

Analysis in terms of major plant nutrients differs with each species of weed, many of which, however, are usually found in most consignments. Rich in the most readily decayed ingredients, the non-fibrous organic matter of these mixed, rootless algae leaves little residue in soils after the first year, but quickly breaks down to release to plants approximately 23 to 28 lb. of potash, 85 lb. of nitrogenous compounds, 2 to 2¼ lb. of phosphorus and 50 lb. of lime per ton. Its high potash content puts seaweed into the same category as bracken, and the use of both is a long-term method of remedying a deficiency of this element in soils; or of stepping-up the analysis of compost for potash-loving crops, such as tomatoes and potatoes. Farmyard manure supplies little over half as much potash though 3 to 4 lb. more of both phosphorus and nitrogen per ton. A minor snag is the salt content of seaweed, 25 to 35 lb. per ton. Sodium chloride has been found to affect mildly the function of plant carbohydrates. To leach it, washing with fresh water (especially when seaweed is to be applied to heavy or clay soils which are only slowly leached) is often recommended but rarely done. Even on such soils, it may indeed be a disadvantage to wash the weed for some crops, such as asparagus, turnips, swedes and mangolds, which may benefit from a little salt.

Seaweed is commonly used on market gardens in coastal areas, at the rate of 50 tons per acre per year, for practically all crops to which farm yard manure is normally applied. It is usually cultivated in not less than two months before a crop is set, otherwise it has a tendency to make some plants smell or taste unpleasantly. For potatoes, which do well on its high potash, it should be cultivated or dug in, preferably after the previous harvest or during autumn; failure to 'set', 'waxiness' or poor keeping-quality of tubers can occur if seed is sown in undecomposed seaweed. Twenty tons of seaweed to the acre (although up to 30 tons are often used), with 2 cwts. of ground rock phosphate, is a good dressing for potatoes and will usually produce, on good soil, a weight of tubers about equal to those of a crop which received the same quantity of farmyard manure. Well-rotted dung at 10 tons to the acre, with fresh seaweed at 7 tons, makes a good dressing for tomatoes, the slower-decaying constituents of the muck being especially valuable in carrying the crop over the complete growing season. This 'compound' may not, however, be free of weed seeds or disease organisms, contributed by the dung, as seaweed alone is. One of the disadvantages of seaweed if cultivated in, is that its value (in terms of plant foods released) may be expended, because of quick decay, before a long-maturing crop, such as brassicas, is pushed through to harvesting. Because of this, and the dubious effect on the soil's humus content as a result of cultivating in highly nitrogenous and readily decomposable organic matter, the writer prefers to get slower breakdown and avoid crop tainting by mulching seaweed for all crops, or alternatively, by using it in bulk compost-making.

Seaweed, always scarce, is most economically reserved for the potash-lovers in the rotation, but can be applied as a surface dressing to practically all vegetable crops and up to 6 inches thick for soft fruits, etc. The inevitable snag is its tendency to dry out and become hard and brittle on the surface. It thereby restricts to some extent the free use of garden machinery, except the rotary cultivator, which can later be used to churn the mulch under the surface. However, the weed-strangling effect of seaweed compensates for this and, in any case, the surface of a thick mulch can be kept moist, and free of flies and smell, by covering it with a thin layer of hay or chaffed straw.

The main ingredients for success when composting seaweed, one of the most violent disintegrators known, are preliminary draining (if it is fresh from the sea), incorporating it with vegetable matter supplying absorbent material and fibre, mixing it well in, or keeping it in thin layers, to avoid insulating one part of the heap from another. If spread about a foot thick for 48 hours before the compost heap is made, seaweed loses about half its moisture content by evaporation and drainage; thus can be avoided the slimey, smelly mess, like silage effluent or the sediment from the bottom of a barrel of black molasses, which results from the putrefaction of sodden, airless heaps. With a blended mixture of semi-dry seaweed, and equal quantities by bulk of straw or bracken (for fibre and aeration) and the usual consignment of vegetable wastes, less activator is required than usual, because of high nitrogen in the weed; half the normal quantity of farmyard manure is sufficient to get the heap off to a good start, and even less is required if the proportion of seaweed goes up, as it can do with composting experience, to half that of the total vegetable matter. The heap should be built not more than about 6 feet wide, and high, on a thick, open foundation with one ventilation hole to every 3 square feet of surface, and left unwatered for at least the first month. A turning is then usually found necessary, to bring into the inside of the heap the brittle and dried weed at its surface and sides; no ventilation hole is needed after turning. Within three months, from first building (often much less, but depending to some extent on other ingredients used), the heap breaks down well into a fine, friable mixture. Such compost, which originally contained up to 50 per cent of seaweed, has been found especially good for tomato potting mixtures, and for all the potash-lovers. No ceiling limit has been found by the writer for the amount which can be applied to general garden crops (although it would undoubtedly be too rich for some plants, like alpines, which have very weak appetites).

One traditional (anaerobic) composting method was to mix together equal quantities of seaweed and soil, and to heap them for several weeks. The Indore process is an improvement on this, but it is still useful where organic matter is extremely scarce, and indicates a safe method of storing seaweed (well under a thick coating of earth) for later composting or direct use. In general, it should be used as soon as possible: after a time, dumped seaweed indicates the direction of the prevailing wind far more effectively than it indicates wet or dry weather.

STRAW

Only about 11 lb. of nitrogen, 20 to 25 lb. of potash and 4 lb. of phosphoric acid per ton of corn straw, locked up inside a resistant, waterproof 'varnish' of clavatin, are left behind by the grain for which we grow cereal crops. On the orthodox farm, particularly the stockless one, this is often considered insufficient return for labour spent elsewhere than behind the combine harvester, where stubble and straw are turned under in the course of ordinary autumn ploughing. Stacks are sent up in smoke in the corners of fields in some districts, while straw for litter is expensive in others. All this is mainly because of its high transport costs and 'low manurial value', only incidentally because 3 to 4 tons of this high-cellulose material, very low in nitrogen, when cultivated in, can lose by twelve weeks' nitrogen-starvation of growing crops more than it gains from added plant foods, on the short-term view.

Analysis for plant nutrients is, however, of less importance to the organic gardener than to his orthodox counterpart. Straw, though poor in NP and K, can solve many of his problems, and has a multiplicity of uses other than in the compost heap, or surrounding it (when baled). It makes useful litter for domestic animals and poultry although it is more expensive than is sawdust; it is one of the best drainers and improvers of heavy or clay soils and can be used in any of a hundred and one different ways, from insulating strawberries against dirt and tender plants from frost, to stuffing the scarecrow.

The main concern of the organic gardener who buys straw by the bale, is how to use it most economically. What the country composter often needs, however, is a method of using the vast bulk of straw which he sometimes gets, for nothing, and which can stand about for years before it disappears in small quantities into the conventional compost heap. It can be used as a mulch for vegetable beds or herbaceous crops, but takes six months or more to rot into a fertile soil, and when cultivated in, needs per ton the nitrogen in 7 cwts. of poultry manure, if nitrogen robbery is to be avoided. Disposal proves no problem to proud septic tank and cesspool owners; a heap of straw, used as a sort of filling station on the road from sewage disposal to soil fertility, will absorb vast quantities of urine and liquid sludge pumped over it (and lightly covered with more straw), and breaks down well over a period of several months. Another way to use vast quantities of straw and to get from it a semi-rotted material about as good as farmyard manure, is to use a modified form of the orthodox recipe and method for making 'artificial farmyard manure', evolved over thirty years ago at Rothamsted.

Basing calculations on the treatment of 5 tons of straw, which stacks in a heap roughly 20 to 25 feet long, 10 feet wide and 6 to 7 feet high, the main requirements for the modified 'artificial farmyard manure' process are: up to 4,000 gallons of water, just over the $3\frac{1}{2}$ cwt. of nitrogen in about a ton of poultry manure (the best activator because it favours the cellulose-decomposing bacteria, although nitrogenous organics other than this can be used) and $3\frac{1}{4}$ to 5 cwt. of ground chalk or limestone. The heap should start, on a rough base of brushwood or thick hedge-clippings to ensure good aeration, over agricultural drain-pipes placed herring-bone fashion, or drainage channels cut in the same pattern in the soil foundation. It should not be more than 10 feet wide, and eight or nine layers of well-shaken straw, each 9 inches to a foot thick, will bring it to the required height of about 7 feet. As each layer of straw is lightly added to the heap, it should be *thoroughly* wetted; on top of each of the first and second layers should be forked or sprinkled a fifth or sixth of the total quantity of ground chalk or limestone to be used, on the third layer, about a quarter of the total quantity of poultry manure, and on the fourth more neutralizer. The heap, partially built, should then be left for two days to allow fungi to open their attack. On the third day, more layers of straw, each lightly built and thoroughly watered, should be added, with between them, neutralizer and activator alternately (poultry manure on the fifth and seventh layers and the topmost, ground chalk or limestone on the sixth and eighth).

A thin layer of straw should be added to complete the heap, which then needs final watering.

After ten days to a fortnight, by which time the temperature should rise to 130° F. (55° C.) to 160–170° F. (70–76° C.), the heap should be thoroughly saturated from a slow hose, from the top, but not with sufficient water to cause much to run from the base. After a further two to three weeks, during which the heap will have compacted to 4 or 5 feet high and its temperature slowly fallen, it should be moistened at intervals (but with less water than at the start of the process), if it has tended to dry out by evaporation beneath the top crust of a foot or so of straw, which remains undecomposed.

Periodic watering of the heap may be necessary for the first three months in all but the wettest districts. A turning, made during the third month, makes for a finer end-product, although complete homogeneous decomposition, to the point where all traces of the original straw have gone, will take several months. The most important points are, aeration, light building and adequate watering, especially during the first half of the 'composting' period. It is no use trying this method where there is a shortage of water, unless the liquid sludge or the urine from the cowshed sump can be diluted to provide activator and moisture in one go. Pre-soaking of straw which is only slowly absorbent is a considerable advantage. This can be done with water from a slow hose, or with a pierced pipeline and tap by means of drip irrigation at low pressure over several days to saturate baled straw before wires are cut and the heap is built.

The modified 'artificial farmyard manure' process has often some, usually many, and sometimes all of the disadvantages of any 'solo' recipe and method, but after five or six months from the date of building, the heap (excepting the outside foot layer) should yield about 20 cubic yards of partially decomposed organic matter, which can be cut down with a hay-knife easier than pulled apart with a muck-fork. This very slow decay of straw, and other heap ingredients, into something not unlike decayed farmyard manure, is less important than the fact that the end-product only vaguely resembles what the good organic gardener means by 'compost', and can still cause nitrogen starvation if cultivated in too early. For these reasons, it is better used as a mulch, applied in the autumn, except for heavy clay on which cropping can be put off for a few weeks and 10 tons to the acre cultivated in gives the improvement in drainage and aeration which makes this delay, and the extra labour for cultivation, worth while. Turned into ordinary soil at the same rate, it usually gives better results in the second than the first year, due to further break-down and stabilization of the carbon/nitrogen ratio.

The writer has used extensively straw decomposed in this way, applied always as a mulch in the autumn, a foot or more thick for all fruit trees, and less than 3 inches deep for most garden vegetable crops.

Indore compost made from a variety of vegetable wastes, of which a little straw is only one, has obvious advantages over 'artificial farm-yard manure' to those who have tried both, apart from the greater ease with which it is made. The 'artificial farmyard manure' process is therefore recommended only for those who wish to deal with a great bulk of straw; otherwise, conventional composting means a better end-product with less danger of trouble in the heap, or the soil to which it is applied.

The value of cereal straw (including old thatch), also hay, which is more resistant to decomposition but can be treated in much the same way, lies mainly in fungal and bacterial food. However, both hay and straw are good improvers of poor soil, and their value is not diminished by weathering or rotting, so that they can be dumped for long periods without loss, until needed to swell the ordinary crop wastes and weeds which go to make Indore compost. Both straw and hay should be thoroughly wetted (soaked in the old water-butt over-night, or better still, for forty-eight hours, or sluiced several times from a bucket by a thatcher's method) before going into the small compost heap at the rate of 25 per cent or less by bulk of the entire mixed vegetable wastes. They should not be used in great quantity or heating may be slow, nor should they be used dry, except to soak up excess moisture in a large bulk of lawn mowings, greengrocers' wastes, seaweed or similar stuff. Chaffing is not normally necessary.

Chaff and cavings can be used for conventional compost-making in much the same way as straw. They often contain weed seeds, how-ever, which means that maximum temperatures must be obtained in the heap if the fine compost to which they contribute is to be trouble-free when used for seed and potting work.

WATER WEED

On warm waters as far apart as Florida and Bihar, Water Hyacinth (*Eichhornia crassipes*) appears, as fast as froth on badly poured beer, in 10 tons of organic matter per water-acre, to present costly fishing and navigation problems. The fact that this picturesque weed will not survive an English winter is perhaps a mixed blessing, but in the Channel Islands, it has been cultivated, in a lagoon which receives the effluent from sewage settling tanks, to be composted with sludge, the growing medium, and habitation refuse in aerobic fermentation bins. A description of methods by which Water Hyacinth can be composted by the ordinary gardener, would be out of place in this book, except to mention that the temptation is usually to put too much of it into the heap, when it is still green; it should be drained and wilted for about three weeks for best results. We have no fast-growing Water Hyacinth (indeed, our adopted Russian Comfrey (*Symphytum peregrinum*) is the only temperate-climate plant, which has equivalent growth speed), but there is, of course, the revenue of water weeds from Britain's thousands of rivers, streams and water-filled quarries which, like by-pass verges and roundabouts, are never taken into account by those who laboriously insist that 'we cannot feed ourselves'.

This buckshee crop repays well those who have time to drag it from adjacent water with the aid of a long rake or fork, or to cut it with a short-handled scythe if the water is not too deep to be waded in. It is useful bulk organic matter for compost-making, and contains in some cases 2 to 3 per cent of nitrogen, 3 to 5 per cent of potash, 2 per cent of phosphates, plus algae and animal matter contributed by sundry water inhabitants.

The traditional method of composting water weed was to mix it with an equal quantity of good soil to produce a well-rotted manure after several months of low-temperature and mainly anaerobic decomposition. The main snag was that of having to provide sufficient soil to prevent the moist, slimy weed from slipping in the stack. The modified Indore process, in which water weed is one of several heap-ingredients, is a more complicated composting method, but gives distinctly better results.

Water weed, like seaweed, should be drained and wilted for about 48 hours (preferably on the quarry or river bank, to save handling heavy and useless water) before it is put into the ordinary compost heap. About the maximum quantity that the beginner can safely use is 30 per cent by bulk of the total vegetable wastes. The proportion can be increased to as much as 50 per cent or more by bulk, in the old hand's heaps, if the weed is (as it should be) mixed with dry stuff, such as straw, cavings, sawdust or chipwood. If other ingredients used are moisture-rich, swill may be produced instead of compost, and this danger must be guarded against. It is never serious where little water weed is used, but otherwise may be so unless dry stuff is added to soak up the moisture not drained away or evaporated before the heap is built. In the writer's experience, it pays to make a 'water weed heap' not more than 8 feet wide and 6 feet high, to give it one ventilation hole to every 4 square feet of surface, and to turn it after three to four weeks, when the brittle, dry or sprouted weed from the surface and outsides can be put into the centre. A three-month composting period usually covers complete breakdown and the heap yields a valuable, and in some cases, weed-free dividend for the organic garden. Uncomposted water weed, which is smelly and may cause crop-taint, should not be cultivated into vegetable beds. It can be mulched, but dries out quicker than does seaweed, is more fibrous and, elsewhere than under fruit trees or perennial crops, may cause serious restrictions when hoeing or cultivating. Certain species of weed seem inevitably to be accompanied by nettle seedlings.

CHAPTER IV

DISEASED MATERIALS AND SPECIAL COMPOSTS

Section I: Composting Diseased or Noxious Materials

In nature, plants are nourished, directly or indirectly, partly or wholly, on their own decayed remains, as in an oak wood. The organic gardener applies this plant food economy in many respects in the garden, but the possible spread of disease is one of his main arguments against mulching or cultivating in raw organic matter exclusively, and in favour of composting. His use of the compost heap to reduce diseased vegetable matter and germ-carrying manures to valuable 'clean' plant foods is based on the sterilizing effect of the heat produced by complete decay, and the antagonistic action of enormous numbers of beneficial organisms against pathogens (disease-producers), a skirmish which, could we see it, would make World War II look like a garden party.

At its maximum in the inside, particularly the very middle, of the good-sized, well-made compost heap, the heat is the same as that in an electric soil sterilizer. Some pathogenic organisms can survive this temperature, one is even capable of regeneration after burning, just as some raspberry seeds may remain viable after they have been through the jam-making process. Most succumb, however, under the moist conditions in the heap, at temperatures which are normally much higher than those necessary in the orthodox hot-water treatment of bulbs, roots, seeds, stools, etc., immersed for given periods in water, or a hot current of air, at a temperature which is fatal to the foe, but harmless to the host. The strawberry mite (*Tarsonemus pallidus*), chrysanthemum eelworm (*Aphelenchoides ritzemabosi*) and the stem eelworm of phloxes are all dead after twenty minutes at 110° F. (43° C.), so is *Anguillulina dipsaci*, the nematode that attacks narcissus bulbs, after three hours at this same temperature. *Bacterium tracheiphilium* which causes cucumber wilt (fortunately not wide-spread in the British Isles), gives up the ghost within twenty-five minutes at 125° F. (52° C.). Both the hyphae and spores of potato blight (*Phytopthora infestans*), on or in potato tubers, are killed at a temperature of 104° F. (40° C.) in a warm current of air.

Disease organisms and weed seeds are most likely to survive in the outside 'crust' of the compost heap (a few inches at the top and sides, more at the corners if these are not kept sufficiently moist), which is colder and therefore decomposes more slowly than the guts of the heap. To make sure that trouble-makers are subjected to highest temperatures at the earliest moment during the composting process, a good precaution is to place seedling weeds and seriously diseased materials, such as 'blighted' tomato foliage, well in the centre of the heap when it is first made. Club-rooted brassica stalks can go straight into the large heap, but for extra safety, the small-scale composter is advised to chop them (well away from the vegetable bed), to place them in the middle of the heap when it is made, and replace them there during the turning operation. If necessary, keep them together in a home-made wire-netting container (like the basket in which potato chips are suspended during frying). The heap in which much diseased material is being composted should be turned at least once, a month from the date on which it was built, and preferably a second time, three to four weeks later. On each occasion the outside edges, split down with a spade or fork, should be put well in the centre. When the heap is finally ready for use, it pays to peel off any still un-decomposed stuff and put it through a second heap or use it for the foundation of another heap.

The compost heap is normally at its hottest during the first month from building, when temperatures in the bin or pit are usually well above the 112° F. (44° C.) at which most weed seeds are killed and in the larger heap, often up to the 160–170° F. (70–76° C.) which most viruses cannot stand for more than ten minutes. Temperatures rarely exceed these points after the turning has been made, and occasionally do not even reach them in the beginner's heaps. However, tempera-ture control is only half the story: it is often the end-product of the small, slow-heating heap which demonstrates most convincingly that biological control is probably the more effective weapon against pests and disease-producers (though not against weed seeds).

Many growers have composted tomato haulm black with blight and roots infested with eelworm, and applied it to tomato houses again and again with complete success. Indeed, many have recommended that compost made with some diseased material, such as club-rooted brassicas, should deliberately be used to fertilize the same or another susceptible crop, primarily to act as a sort of specific for infected soils. This seems to have proved effective in many cases, but, as N. P. Burman, B.Sc., F.I.M.L.T., Ph.D., stated in the Soil Association's Information Bulletin (No. 47, January 1952, p. 8, item 71): 'I am inclined to think that compost made from healthy brassicas or any other crop would be just as effective. The micro-organisms which feed on the club-root disease organisms also feed on harmless micro-organisms and, therefore, they are liable to be encouraged just as much by the large numbers of harmless organisms which multiply in an ordinary compost heap as by the relatively few club-root disease organisms in a heap made of diseased materials.'

In spite of the fact that growers are 'sailing close to the wind' by conducting experiments of this sort, their results are interesting. In the Spring, 1948, issue of *Mother Earth* (p. 16), E. B. Balfour reported on the growing of completely healthy brassicas on land which had (deliberately) been given applications of compost made from as much club-root-infected material as could be collected locally by a Lancashire gardener. The excellent results obtained were observed and the earlier report corroborated by the same writer over a year later in the same publication, which also carried the observation by J. Carter, that he had no reason to regret the use of club-rooted brassicas, docks in seed, thistles or willow-herb, in his compost heaps.

In the Autumn, 1947, number of *Mother Earth* (p. 32), appeared an account of some brief experiments, involving in one way or another, the John Innes Horticultural Institute and a Rothamsted official. They were carried out on the composting of tomato plants, carefully lifted from the ground to retain roots, badly infected with virus. In a one-year comparison for which records are available, this compost was found to give a higher percentage of 'healthy' tomato plants of two varieties than did the same quantity, 20 tons to the acre, of horse manure. Virus was found still infecting the roots of some of the compost-treated plants, *but did not appear to affect adversely the vigour or health of them or their yield.* (Many viruses are, of course, not killed at temperatures which few weed seeds survive, and it is interesting to note that, according to the editor of the reporting journal, the compost used in this experiment was 'crudely' made.) E. F. Watson, O.B.E., A.M.I.M.E., has similarly reported (*Mother Earth*, Spring,

1948, p. 29) greatly reduced incidence of virus disease in trials with tomatoes and zinnias, fertilized with compost made from both virus-diseased and healthy materials. *The Grower*, 28th February 1948, reported that in the opinion of the experts a temperature of 160° F. (70° C.) in a well-made compost heap would effect the destruction of any potential disease.

That as well as short-circuiting the cycle of many plant diseases, it is possible to handle smelly pig manure next to a girls' school without the risk of a Ronald Searlean uprising, or human excrement without offensiveness or danger, is some measure of the efficiency of good composting methods. The degree of cleanliness and purity which can be obtained in the large-scale composting of sewage and night soil, has been demonstrated in scientifically controlled experiments, notably those reported at length and in detail by James Cameron Scott, in *Health and Agriculture in China*, and by J. P. J. van Vuren (South Africa) in *Soil Fertility and Sewage* (both published by Faber and Faber). These writers report no fly-breeding, nor survival of hookworm and ascaris in carefully controlled compost heaps (this in two of the worst areas in the world for intestinal infections).

No official trials as comprehensive as these have yet been undertaken in England, to find out to what extent there is, or is not, survival of disease organisms in properly composted night soil. However, in *Our Answer on the Land*, No. 4 (published by the Albert Howard Foundation of Organic Husbandry—now merged with the Soil Association Ltd.), Dr. Werner Grussendorf stated that he found no *Bacterium coli* in samples of his own compost made (in Germany) with night soil and nutrias manure as two ingredients. *B. coli* is used as an 'indicator of pollution', by sewage or manure, of water supplies derived from springs or wells. It is not a pathogenic organism, nor a normal inhabitant of the soil—where it usually dies out over a period of time—but it is a normal inhabitant of human and animal intestinal tracts, appears therefore in animal and human excreta and may be present in dried blood, which often contains intestinal remains from slaughter-houses. This particular bacterium is absent, completely or almost entirely, from compost made under conditions of high-temperature fermentation and from sewage sludge treated by (high-temperature) drying, pulverizing and digesting. But its absence can only be guaranteed by analysis of each individual sample of organic compost or manure: therefore, the use of all but artificial fertilizers on land adjacent to wells, from which a municipal water supply is derived, has in some cases, been justifiably forbidden. This prohibition need not alarm the general composter: it is, in such cases (few and far between) a small price to pay for a 'safe' water supply.

Not the danger of perpetuating diseases, but fastidiousness, is the main bugbear in civilized countries, particularly in the use of night soil. This often presents acute disposal problems for the country house with an earth closet, septic tank or cesspool, and on the market garden where a dozen men fond of beer and with healthy appetites are working in a limited space, in England, as well as in America and Canada. Valuable time is often lost in deep-burying an unmentionable commodity, which decays slowly and anaerobically in the subsoil and sometimes checks growth on the surface of precious land. If human excrement must be buried (in other words, lost), it should be allowed to decompose in the presence of air, just below the surface of the soil on the waste patch of ground. No smell is then produced after the first few minutes and decomposition is quick and complete. Direct use of unprocessed faeces or urine on cultivated land is *not* recommended under any circumstances.

To compost night soil or sewage (from the private house), thoroughly and at high temperatures, however, makes it safe for garden use, saves labour and space for deep burying and the cost of purchased activators. The main snag is that caused by the residues of disinfectants, deodorants and detergents brought into the septic tank or cesspit in water from sinks, baths and flush pans. Only very high concentrations of these will seriously reduce the value of the sludge or shut down the fermentation process completely in the compost heap. Ordinary soapy water does not appear to do much harm, especially if sterilizing chemicals can be reduced to a minimum. Newspaper, in the small quantities used in place of the print-free toilet roll, will not be harmful because of printers' ink, and chemicals can be dispensed with altogether in the country earth closet. Soil or an alternative 'soak' in place of a chemical is all that is required to eliminate smell and prevent fly infestation of one of the best activators, without any of the disadvantages of specialized microbiological activity because of chemical sterilization in the bucket. (The contents of the 'chemical closet' in which a fluid composed of the cheaper tar oil disinfectants, mainly phenols, has been used to mask smells and remove any infection risk, is unsuitable for composting. This material should be buried as directed by the makers, as it will contain creosote as well and might never decay properly in the heap.)

Management of the chemical-changed-to-earth closet is simple. The best method is to start by putting a twist of straw, like a bird's nest, and a shovelful of soil in the bottom of the empty bucket. Further sprinklings of earth should then be added from a handy pailful, every time after the closet's use. Earth is a very efficient soak, but heavy; lighter sawdust, chaff and wood ash, make for easier handling of the full bucket—an important consideration if the emptier is not robust. Experience indicates the amount of any given material which is a necessary addition: if the 'soak' is added in light sprinklings, just sufficient to keep a dry surface and prevent smell, there need be no more frequent emptying of the bucket than usual, or than can be made an operation to coincide with routine composting. The bucket, gradually filled without splashing or offensiveness, is finally emptied (direct on to a compost heap in course of construction at that time, or on a storage heap) and washed out thoroughly with clean water, ready for the whole process to be repeated.

As an activator, the semi-liquid contents of the bucket can be poured over layers of vegetable wastes when making ordinary compost. No ground chalk or limestone need be added to the heap if wood-ash has been used as a 'soak', or a little less than usual if good earth, as the mixture you get from the bucket is similar to the late Sir Albert Howard's 'urine/earth'; it provides both activator and base in one go. It should preferably be used immediately on emptying, poured from the centre of the heap outwards to within 3 or 4 inches of the sides, with the swill water from the bucket-cleaning operation to provide any necessary moisture for the heap (which should have a final coating of earth). Night soil is not compact and easily measurable by bulk as are most other manures, and experience must accurately judge the quantity necessary for efficient activation without smelliness. All smell should disperse within a matter of hours. Start with too little night soil rather than too much in the heap, to be on the safe side. Things to avoid are urine draining from the base: an inch or so of sawdust or peat should be used to soak it up if this happens; unnecessary slopping over the sides of the heap which should be turned at least once, and preferably twice, at monthly intervals from the time of building. The contents of the chamber-pot can be dealt with in much the same way.

When there is no compost heap in the making to take the emptyings from the earth closet, these can safely be stored for later use.

Build up a 'storage heap' of layers of earth and straw or peat, 4 feet square and about $1\frac{1}{2}$ to 2 feet high, pour the bucket contents on to the middle of this and add a little more earth and straw. Repeat the last part of the process whenever the bucket is emptied, until such time as the semi-decomposed mixture, and one or two bucketfuls of fresh night soil for rapid activation purposes, can be added to a good-sized compost heap in course of construction. Weekly emptying of the bucket enables the small, binned compost-heap to be built up in sections (by the method described in Chapter II), but this is better avoided, unless it can be done carefully, in case of smell or fly-breeding.

The hundreds of gallons of sludge and effluent from the domestic cesspit or septic tank are best emptied direct into an otherwise fairly dry compost heap, or, if they contain much soap, etc., poured over a large heap of straw (as far away from human habitation as possible), and covered with more straw or vegetable matter, to allow time for the breakdown by 'weathering' of phenols and other chemical residues. In many cases, this is the 'composting' system used; where ground slopes away from the surface of the cesspit, effluent is drained and sludge tipped direct on to a heap of straw (or the conventional compost mixture), which is then turned down on a sort of terrace system until finally mature. Processed sewage sludge is discussed in Appendix I.

Methodical building for highest temperatures is the key to composting offensive substances, not only night soil and sewage, but also fish offal, which comes into the same category of 'objectionable stuff'. The only places where you can get fish offal are near the coast and in some local fishmongers' shops, but not all. In the London area, and in several large cities in England, there is organized collection of fishmongers' wastes by private firms, for the production of high-grade feeding-stuffs. Piracy by individuals might not altogether be a good thing in these areas; outside them there is everything to be said for weekly or twice-weekly trips to the local fishmonger by the methodical composter (not the unmethodical: a visit missed and both fish and gardener get in very bad odour).

Raw fish offal is too rich for tender roots, and too attractive to cats, for safety if used direct. Composting clamps down and quietens it very effectively, however, whilst gaining maximum value in quick activation from the nitrogen in its readily decayed proteins, and its high phosphorus content. All smell disperses quickly if the proportion of offal used is limited to one part by bulk to not less than three parts of mixed vegetable wastes, and the fly menace is avoided by keeping the offal well in the centre of the heap. One turning at the end of the first month is usually sufficient to maintain aeration and speed decomposition of tough heads and tails which may have lodged in the bottom half of the heap.

The insides that do not go as giblets when table birds are dressed for market on the poultry farm need cause no more trouble than fish wastes and serve much the same purpose in the compost heap, provided that this is methodically built. The necessity is for a good composting method with, for choice, straw, roadside cleanings, spent tan bark, or a little sawdust, plus some poultry manure. The writer has tried a mixture of all these: a heap built up in a layer sequence of: 4 inches of rough foundation, 1 inch of poultry manure ($\frac{1}{2}$ inch or less would have been sufficient, if superphosphate-treated), 2 inches of dampened straw, 1 inch of chicken offal topped with a sprinkling of ground chalk or limestone (sufficient to make the surface white), and a final layer of mixed vegetable matter containing some sawdust and spent tan bark. One ventilation hole was made to each 3 square feet of heap surface and a turning was given at the end of the fifth week. This experimental heap, and others, gave satisfactory results in terms of good quality compost, despite many feather skeletons still remaining at the end of the fourth month.

'Dirt is matter in the wrong place': the right place is in the purifying compost heap, provided that it is carefully managed. It is easy to perpetuate viruses and other troubles and to depress beneficial organisms by bad methods, illustrated by the profusion of weeds and 'blighted' foliage which often follows the application of semi-decayed vegetation from the rubbish dump in the corner of many a garden. Care must be exercised when handling the objectionable stuff already mentioned in this chapter, also the small quantities of fish and meat which come from the kitchen, especially to the town garden—one of many in a long row. Even then, only a wire-netting screen and rat-traps arranged like war-time beach defences, will satisfy some neighbours, until they thoroughly understand what is going on, and the safety and sanitation of the process are demonstrated. The short-circuiting of the disease-cycle does not involve the use of special composting methods, but greater care than usual is necessary to make sure that partial decay and inadequate heating shall not allow infected material, also weed seeds and roots, to pass on unchanged.

Section II: Special Composts and Potting Mixtures

Members of the vegetable kingdom, naturally growing among their own decayed remains, often use those remains, as pine trees do their needles, as weapons against other vegetation. The necessity for this, as one means to plants' survival, is largely ruled out by cultivation and weed control in the ordinary garden, and reduced to a large extent under methods of surface cultivation. So also is the disease risk by composting, but because of problems arising from domestication (monoculture in the orchard and the greenhouse—acres down to one plant rather than a mixed culture) the composter often finds it convenient to return to some crops their own wastes after treatment. For example, prunings, rotten fruit and leaves can go into a 'special' compost for the orchard, haulm or bines into another for tomatoes or potatoes. (Always, of course, as much other waste vegetable matter as possible should go into the heap: to make a good 'mixture' and especially on the market garden, to supply the equivalent quantities of nutrients removed in the fruit, seeds, foliage or roots for which the crops are grown.) Many growers claim that such composts have special virtues. Many crops certainly appear to flourish on their own decayed remains, but, in the writer's opinion, not more so than on good ordinary compost, made from mixed vegetable and animal wastes fermented at temperatures which are lethal to pathogenic organisms and weed seeds. There seems little point in making such 'special' composts deliberately, unless time and labour are saved.

Ordinary compost made from mixed vegetable wastes is normally on the slightly alkaline side, a pH between 7·2 and 7·7 being common in the heap after three to four months from making. Although, in the writer's experience, such composts have given good results on rhododendrons, ericas, gentians and strawberries, many growers prefer a special compost for these and other acid lovers.

The only way to get an acid compost is to omit the neutralizer (limestone, chalk, wood ash, etc.) from the heap, or to reduce the quantity used. By this method a pH of 6·1 to 6·4 is easily obtained: M. C. Rayner and W. Neilsen Jones (in *Problems in Tree Nutrition*, Faber) record this reaction in 'compost' (for conifer seedlings) made from 50 per cent hardwood sawdust, 50 per cent straw, plus dried blood supplying nitrogen at one-hundredth the air-dry weight of these materials; the writer, also, has recorded it in compost made without lime but with 25 per cent of seaweed put into the heap to speed breakdown of September-cut bracken, straw and mixed weeds. (Normally, a large quantity of one heap-ingredient should be avoided: to put no chalk or limestone into the heap containing much lawn mowings, or similar close-packing materials with a high moisture content, is asking for trouble in the form of putrefaction: slow, airless decay, which can easily be avoided by aiming at a good mixture of materials). To omit the neutralizer from the well-made heap of mixed vegetable wastes normally gives rise to somewhat slow decomposition and fermentation at temperatures below the normal maximum, but nothing more serious, for carbonic acid is the only acid produced in such a heap. You have to wait a little longer than usual, but you get, without trouble, a pH of 6·0, sometimes lower, in an end-product especially useful for most of the lime-haters. It is, however, difficult to make compost with a reaction much below pH 6·0. The only solution to the problem of obtaining an acid potting mixture, for the trio of lime-hating Alpines (for which little compost is required in any case, as it is too rich), and some other plants, is to mix slightly acid or ordinary compost with acid peat (down to pH 4·0) and loam made without chalk or limestone. For ordinary use on cultivated land on which acid-lovers are to be grown, lime-free compost can be supplemented with raw vegetable matter such as green manure (see Appendix II), to keep down the pH of the soil.

Compost for potting mixtures should preferably be taken from the inside of the mature heap (once turned), sieved in order to get rid of any stones and large fragments of decaying material and then mixed with sand, loam, peat or other potting-mixture ingredients. This mixture of materials is used mainly in order to economize on always scarce compost, and to create the best possible conditions for aeration and drainage, but also to avoid over-stimulating tender growth. Most seedlings thrive from the word 'go' on sieved Indore compost, put straight into the frame or tray; brassicas get the best possible start in it, show-size melons, pumpkins and marrows can be grown from seed in neat compost, or round (not on) the compost heap and trained over it; old-fashioned geraniums, from cuttings started and grown in pure compost (replaced every three years, otherwise heavily top-dressed in the town window-box) can be persuaded to give from end to end of the season blooms 18 inches in circumference, the envy of the neighbourhood; and ordinary pot bulbs in pure compost tend to give much better flowers the second year. To use 'neat' Indore compost as a growing medium for some young seedlings is, however, equivalent to giving an adult's helping of steak pie and plum pudding to a baby, apart from being wasteful. Alpines, which evolved to take their nourishment from thin, poor, mountain soils, can stand only very little compost in a standard potting mixture such as seven parts of loam, four of neutral peat or leaf-mould, and three of sharp sand. Tomato seedlings, started in compost rich in available nitrates, may produce so much strong leaf growth that the first truss of fruit is missed (although such a diet will often pull round a weak plant, transplanted into a 10-inch pot or into the top of a compost heap). The potting mixture required for such plants is one with a weaning food value.

Compost is generally used at the rate of 50 per cent or less by bulk of other ingredients in most potting mixtures. Thus equally good results are obtained, if not better, than those with 'neat' compost, without danger of the equivalent of a bilious attack in young plants, and a saving is made on a valuable and always scarce material. Compost is put into the potting mixture mainly to provide what, in the John Innes mixtures, for example, would be supplied by available inorganics; neutral horticultural peat or leaf-mould goes in to assist moisture retention and absorption, coarse or sharp, washed sand for drainage, and loam to give the mixture 'body' and to stabilize what would otherwise be too loose a rooting medium. Peat and sand are sold by horticultural suppliers and leaf-mould can be made by the method given on p. 70. To make good loam you need farmyard manure, ground chalk or limestone, and turves, each about a foot thick and 5 inches deep, cut from well-drained weed-free and not acid grassland, between April and June, during the period of lushest grass growth. The turves, with small air spaces between each, should be stacked in layers and well watered on the way up in a heap not more than 7 feet wide and 6 feet high. Between the first and second layers should be placed a 2- to 3-inch thickness of good farmyard manure with plenty of straw litter, for aeration and activation; between the second and third layers, a sprinkling of ground chalk or limestone should be added to stabilize the reaction of the mixture at about pH 6·3. The completed heap, built up of these double-decker sandwiches of turves, activator and neutralizer, and finally covered with a permanent roof of wood or corrugated iron to keep out rain, should be ready for use in the spring. It should then be split down with a spade and well mixed (or put through a mechanical shredder/mixer) to avoid variations in quality, and sieved through a ⅜ inch riddle to remove any undecomposed roots and stones. Worms can be taken out by the same method, but do little or no harm if left in the mixture. Normally they are killed when loam is sterilized. In the writer's opinion, there is absolutely no necessity for sterilization of good loam, provided this comes from healthy, weed-free, organically managed soil.

There is no end to the serviceable seed and potting mixtures which can be used to start off most garden seeds. (In all cases, the loam, compost, peat or leaf-mould used in them should first be put through a ⅜-inch sieve.) The nearest equivalent (without sterilization or added inorganics) to the John Innes mixture is: seven parts of loam to three of ripe Indore compost, two of coarse washed sand and one of peat or leaf-mould. This mixture has been found suitable for tomatoes, lettuces, brassicas, and most flowers, such as sweet williams and stocks, which are normally transplanted. For those seedlings which, started in seed trays, boxes or the cold frame, are later 'potted' on and only finally planted out, a good double mixture is: 1 to 2 parts of ripe compost, 3 to 4 parts of loam, 3 parts of peat, 2 parts of coarse washed sand (up to ⅛ inch), in seed trays, and equal parts of these ingredients in pots. A compound of two parts of ripe compost, one of coarse washed sand, and two of good, organically managed soil, with a double-handful of fine bonemeal to every 10 lb. of this mixture, may be useful where loam is expensive to purchase or produce.

Potting mixtures can be adjusted to suit the area, the grower, his soil and especially the ingredients he has. G. O. Liss (now in New Zealand but formerly of Manor Nurseries, Hampton-in-Arden, Warwickshire) raised Dutch light tomatoes in soil blocks containing 50 per cent of mature compost, 50 per cent of loam, with a 5-inch pot of bonemeal and half this quantity of hoof-and-horn meal added for each barrow-load of the mixture. Lettuces were pricked out at forty to the standard seed tray, filled with a mixture of three parts of loam to one part of mature compost (passed through a ½-inch sieve), with one 5-inch pot of bonemeal only to each barrow-load of the mixture. One 5-inch pot of carbonate of lime was added at the same rate to both mixtures, because of the particular acidity of the loam used. Many other growers use similar mixtures with and without limestone. Mr. Liss, who did not sterilize, recorded that casualties rarely numbered more than 1 per cent amongst his tomato and lettuce seedlings raised in this way.

DISEASED MATERIALS AND SPECIAL COMPOSTS

In *Common-Sense Compost Making* (Faber), Miss Maye E. Bruce gives a useful sequence of mixtures for tomatoes in pots in the small amateur greenhouse. Miss Bruce recommends that plants should be set low in pots half filled with a mixture of five parts of loam, two of compost and one of sand. Three 2-inch top dressings should then be given at intervals during the growing period; the first mixture consisting of: three parts of compost and four of loam; the second: four parts compost and three of loam; the third: five parts of compost and two of loam. A final top dressing of 'neat' compost to top up the pot should be applied when the first truss of fruit has set, and compost put round the pots on the staging when plant roots appear through drainage holes.

Normally, compost straight from the heap (or sieved) is applied as a top dressing or cultivated into glasshouse soils. Occasionally soil may be removed in some cases during conversion to the organic method (see Chapter V), and mixtures of fresh soil, compost, loam, etc., are substituted. James A. Bower, of Messrs. Bower and Pedley, Wisbech, reported in the Autumn 1947 (p. 23) and Winter 1947-8 (p. 23) issues of *Mother Earth*, that 336 bushels of a mixture of seven parts of loam, three of peat, two of grit and two of ripe compost were used to prepare a propagating house which was planted out with tomatoes on June 29th. The results of subsequent treatment of this crop are interesting. The house was divided into quarters when the first truss of fruit had set; two quarters were left without further manuring of any kind, while the remaining two were given additional dressings, one of sulphate of potash, two of a balanced commercial fertilizer and a nitrogenous dressing of dried blood. By 5th September, just under 50 lb. more of fruit had been pulled from the compost-only sections, and final yield figures for these showed 1,344 lb. of fruit, as against 1,160 lb. from those sections which had received additional fertilizer dressings.

The amateur grower particularly is recommended to evolve his own seed and potting mixtures. A simple compound such as equal parts by bulk of garden compost and loam plus a little sand and peat or leaf-mould, seem to give universally good results. Garden compost must never be sterilized either before or after its incorporation in a seed or potting mixture.

CHAPTER V

COMPOST APPLICATION

To compost by the Indore method in the back garden is to produce a different end-product every time a heap is made, for no two heaps are constructed of exactly similar ingredients, are otherwise exactly alike or behave in a like manner. The gardener can try to make good compost but he cannot dictate exactly what it is to be, chemically and microbiologically, after three months. Much of the technical data which exists concerning 'compost' is based on calculations and observations of mixtures such as sawdust and dried blood only, or straw and a chemical activator only, which Sir Albert Howard probably would never have considered as being compost at all. However, sufficient is known of what happens in the ordinary Indore heap to enable the composter, even the beginner, to calculate what quantity of compost he will get from a given heap, when he will get it and how long he can then keep it without risking serious loss of plant nutrients or organic matter. The knowledge of where it is best spent then comes with the composter's experience.

What is obtained from a compost heap, in terms of texture, weight and bulk, depends mainly on what goes in. A heap of miscellaneous ingredients, stacked by the Indore method, usually diminishes over the complete composting period to as little as two-thirds or half its original height. This is why two heaps, sometimes three, can be 'potted on' into a single one for final 'maturing', yet take up no more space than did one of the original heaps when it was first made. A heap consisting mainly of lawn mowings will, of course, shrink to next to nothing in a matter of weeks; that containing much sawdust or chipwood will settle very little.

The speed with which a heap decomposes depends mainly on the materials used but also on the time of year. The good, summer-built heap in a temperate climate usually takes three to four months to break down into compost suitable for ordinary use. The 'solo' heap of lawn mowings activated with the herbal 'Q.R.' compost activator may be ready for use in a matter of weeks, sometimes even days, whilst the mainly sawdust heap will hang around for much longer, usually more than six months, if it is correctly built, or an eternity if incorrectly. In those later-built autumn or winter heaps of dead stems, foliage and leaves (for which the best activator is poultry manure), decomposition is almost arrested during the coldest weather, and decay is never so quick as the puffs of steam from the heap's ventilation holes would seem to indicate. However, breakdown speeds up, especially if the heap is turned, as soon as warmer weather comes to make bacteria and fungi increasingly active, as if to compensate for time lost under frost temperatures.

Some special composts (consisting of leaves, prunings, etc.) made by fruit-growers take as long as two years to mature; however, such delay is unusual. If a really fine compost is required for seed and potting work, the heap's ingredients can be chaffed before composting begins, or the heap can be sieved immediately before the compost is used. If, on the other hand, a rough compost is preferred, as it usually is by the non-diggers for their annual autumn mulch, the heap can be dismantled early, even before it is fully mature.

The original constituents of the 'mature' compost heap (sampled from the inside) are almost or entirely unrecognizable: in about three months they have broken down into a rich compost, sweet-smelling, dark, resembling moist peat, soil and forest humus, of which usually between 50 and 80 per cent will pass a $\frac{1}{2}$-inch sieve and the whole is easier turned or picked up with a spade than with a fork. Such compost has no predictable specific gravity or precise weight; its measurement is therefore tricky. Its weight depends a little on the materials from which it is made, more on its state of decay but most of all on its moisture content. Compost can absorb ten times its own weight of water, a commodity which can therefore be expensively purchased if compost is bought and sold on weight alone. Despite the fact that sale of 'manure' by bulk is illegal, to measure and sell compost by volume rather than weight would obviously be the better standard system—for the purchaser if not the vendor. Most growers, however, calculate that mature three-month compost (of the Indore or back-garden variety; not the uniform commercial stuff) weighs out at from 10 cwt. to 1 ton per cubic yard, and accept 15 cwt. per cubic yard as average.

In the compost heap decay is continuous and in theory will go on until, after a few years, only a minute proportion of relatively stable matter and humus remains. As the heap's bulky organic matter is dispersed, the proportion of plant foods and minerals rises; therefore compost increases in nutrient value with age, during storage for limited periods. Such increase is an advantage if a rich compost is required. However, in general, it does not compensate for the loss of organic matter which is no longer available to feed the soil population or to improve the soil's structure, texture and moisture-holding capacity. Humus is of little use as a food to micro-organisms and other creatures. Compost should therefore be used immediately it is 'mature'. Even if it cannot be cultivated in because plants are occupying the land, it can be applied as a mulch for it does as much good, or more, on the surface of the soil.

Indeed, the greatest value from garden compost is obtained if it is spread over dug soil or lightly forked into the soil. Here, in the presence of air and micro-organisms garden compost completes its decomposition. Compost is wasted if incorporated in the subsoil, out of reach of plant roots and soil organisms, except perhaps in the bottom of a sweet-pea trench, under a first-year rose bush, or for certain purposes of soil improvement (see below). Its value 'percolates' into and throughout the soil, is therefore not lost if compost is applied as a mulch. For those who can make sufficient compost to cover their vegetable beds with a 2-inch dressing every autumn, such a mulch can virtually do away with digging and much other 'routine' soil disturbance, including weeding. Unfortunately, it is not much good trying No-Digging (see Appendix II) unless compost is available in quantity.

The amount of compost which is applied per square yard or per acre each year to ordinarily fertile garden soils depends solely on the quantity available: there is no ceiling limit if compost is unlimited. As there is normally never so much compost as the gardener would wish, especially the beginner whose scrounging technique isn't good, a first essential is to return to the land every bit of waste material, plus any extra that can be brought in, to make up a quantity of decomposed organic matter and plant nutrients at least equivalent to that removed in crops. However, just as half a loaf is, a little compost is better than none, and 3 tons to the acre would seem to be about the minimum for the maintenance of a reasonably varied and numerous soil population. (When compost is as scarce as this, it pays best to apply it to tomatoes, potatoes and brassicas, those greedy crops which contribute the bulk of our green food.) Three tons seems all too little but the beginner does well if he produces 5 tons per acre per year, and to produce much more than this requires luck or the ingenuity of an experienced composter.

Compost of the good Indore variety is usually considered as being at least twice as valuable as farmyard manure, despite the fact that comparison is difficult because the advantages of compost are not solely in its function as a supplier of plant foods. Certainly this assessment is not conclusively borne out by conventional analysis. Analyses by a standard commercial laboratory, of two samples of the writer's 1954 composts made from mixed residues activated with dung, showed:

Soluble Humus	Organic Matter	Total Ash	N	P	K	C/N Ratio
5·46	21·05	79·85	0·86	0·69	4·98	11/1
4·73	22·07	78·47	0·90	0·61	5·30	10/1

These figures are very similar to those recorded during analyses of Sir Albert Howard's heaps at Indore (see *The Waste Products of Agriculture*, O.U.P.), so they are not unusual in any way, but they indicate only a minor part of compost's value. They do not take account of large quantities of minerals and other plant foods locked up in the body protoplasm of micro-organisms or in fragments of undecayed matter, let alone the value of compost as a soil conditioner, moisture retainer, and weed-depressor. More than in such figures, the real value of any given sample of compost would be expressed in terms of numbers of micro-organisms, millions or billions of which would be found per gramme sample of compost. But such analysis figures are at present costly and hard to get, and the composter must rely partly on logic and partly on facts proved by the experiences of others.

On poor land, the more compost that can be applied the better for the first few years, though the quantity required to maintain the standard of crops usually diminishes when treated soil has become really fertile after several years of organic cultivation. However, the quantity applied each year should, where possible, not fall below 10 tons per acre, roughly ⅓ cwt. to 36 square yards. This is usually considered as being a good dressing for fertile land which is not intensively cropped. The rate of application to soils commercially cropped must be correspondingly high, to compensate for the organic matter and nutrients lost in edible crops sold off the land. James A. Bower, of Messrs. Bower and Pedley, Wisbech, writing in the Winter 1947/48 edition of *Mother Earth*, states that he uses each year what he considers to be a heavy annual dressing of 37½ tons of compost to the acre under glass, and about half this quantity on open ground intensively cultivated. (Bower calculates that his compost weighs out at 1½ cubic yards to the ton.) J. L. H. Chase, in his book *Commercial Cloche Gardening* (Faber and Faber) records his opinion that between 10 and 25 tons of compost per acre per year are equivalent to the usual 25 to 50 tons of farmyard manure; he presumably has such a rate of application in mind for land under strip cloche cultivation, where compost is spread only under the glass. Most commercial growers recommend the application of compost at similar rates: about 15 tons per acre per year on open ground, intensively cultivated, and 30 tons under glass, being the figures most commonly quoted. (However, no one has yet found that compost in greater tonnages than this, if such can be economically applied, has been entirely valueless.) Provided that such application to normally healthy garden soils can be maintained, and a good crop rotation is used, there is normally no need for applications of other fertilizers of any sort, organic or inorganic, nor for soil conditioners. However, there are exceptional circumstances. As a penance for his sins, the monocultural man may have to juggle a little with the nutrient content of his compost if he is to avoid deficiencies, because his particular crop, perpetually repeated on the same soil, depletes it of a favoured nutrient. Of course, mucking about with the chemistry of the compost heap can cause trouble, for some minerals can be locked up by others here, as also in the soil. However, the fact that many organic growers raise one or two crops only on well-composted soil, year after year, and some regularly get two to three times as much for their produce, sold wholesale, as do other orthodox growers, illustrates what can be done.

To remedy a deficiency of some element in the soil, a more realistic attitude than the ordinary composter's must be taken. It is true that a good compost made from nettles will make up for some calcium deficiency, but the cost of doing so in time and labour is prohibitive except on a back-garden scale, and even then one has little compost to do more than build up a bit each year. If a soil is definitely deficient in an element (as are some Highland mountain pastures over rock) and has not merely got it locked up by unbalanced dressings of 'artificials' no amount of compost made solely with the crop residues from that area will remedy the deficiency. Assuming that it is worth while to crop such areas (they are few and far between), it is not always economically possible to transport in compost made elsewhere from waste organic matter which contains the required element. In such cases there are alternatives to the use of compost.

Artificial fertilizers possess some distinct advantages over bulky organic manures, such as compost and dung. They are cheaper, for their sale and transport are subsidized, and their effect on soil and crops is visible within a matter of days or weeks, whereas the benefit of compost is cumulative and shows mostly after months or longer. However, if inorganics are used *as expedients*, it should be with the same caution as morphine or cocaine, dangerously habit-forming drugs although they are herbal extracts. The proof of the fertilizer is in the harm that it can do. (It is hard to draw the line between those fertilizers most and least likely to be harmful, but definitely in the first category are the nitrogen-containing salts, sulphate of ammonia and nitrate of soda.) Basic slag and nitro-chalk appear to have least deleterious effect of all the inorganics. However, the organic gardener does not normally need them and, if he is wise, avoids as soon as possible the use of these inorganics, also the potash salts (sulphate, muriate and chloride of potash), urea, calcium cyanamide, superphosphate, etc., and the compound fertilizers which 'have an organic base' but nevertheless almost always contain one or some of these undesirable elements.

A better answer to the deficiency problem than the use of those inorganics which have been treated to speed their rate of solubility or are capable of depressing the soil population, is provided by the natural rocks, unprocessed apart from crushing and pulverizing. Phosphate rock is far less soluble than superphosphate, but it compensates for slow action when used direct by being much more the sort of thing that plants naturally find in the ground. This natural rock, also potash feldspar, greensand, and other mineral rocks, can, of course, be used via the compost heap, in which their breakdown, therefore availability, is speeded up. However, the gardener's aim should be to avoid methods which make such additions necessary. In fertile soils there is an unlimited reserve of plant foods; only a healthy soil population, plus organic matter, moisture and air are needed to bring them into circulation in the quantities required by the crops we grow.

So far as trace elements are concerned, the point to remember (as has already been mentioned), is, that a healthy soil contains *only* a trace of them. Introduce or supply more than that and you get no return for your money or do active harm. Compost keeps up the circulation of the so-called minor, as well as major, minerals, whereas even the most compound of 'artificials' does not take account of all those elements, including minerals, which may be removed in crops to the point at which deficiency shows. On the orthodox garden, a deficiency of a trace element is usually remedied by a method which is often as profitable to the supplier of wonder remedies as are the methods which caused the deficiency. If the organic gardener inherits a deficiency from an orthodox predecessor, or inadvertently creates one himself, he is recommended to supply the required element in seaweed, for example, a good mixed sample of which contains all the known trace elements, or in the form of a natural rock. Magnesium deficiency, which occurs most frequently on light soils and most acutely there during wet seasons, can be remedied by the use of either seaweed (powdered or otherwise) or magnesian dolomitic limestone. Once the deficiency has been remedied, sufficient quantities of organic matter in the form of compost and raw mulches, which act as a buffer between over- and under-supply of minerals, will maintain the level where it is wanted.

The organic gardener obtains from multi-purpose compost, maximum benefits in the maintenance and improvement of soil structure and texture, at no extra cost over the supply and circulation of plant foods. Compost in sufficient quantity, and such effects of its use as the encouragement of a vast population of earthworms, can also much reduce the necessity for watering and virtually do away with artificial aeration of the soil, digging, and some other operations normally considered as 'routine' on any garden. In time, it brings all soils, whatever their original condition, nearer the ideal loam: by lightening, aerating and improving drainage of the heaviest clay; by reducing moisture loss, therefore the leaching of soluble matter and nutrients, and by binding and consolidating the lightest sands. The speed with which improvement shows depends much on the skill of the gardener in treating a particular soil in the most satisfactory way, on the quantity of compost and organic matter used and on the initial condition of the land. Most dramatic results show where conditions are poorest: in town and old kitchen gardens, starved of organic matter, and to a lesser extent on extremely heavy or light soils. On disused aerodromes, or land ruined by open-cast mining and left with that inert subsoil problem which has become more acute since the invention of the bulldozer, the use of 'reclaiming crops', such as *Melilotus alba* which, with the help of an inoculant will grow in pure subsoil, is the obvious first step towards reclamation. The second is composting, of course. Fortunately, we in Britain do not have trouble with the accumulation of salts from irrigation water (except in flood periods such as spring 1953). Although erosion has not yet assumed major proportions in Britain, it is already photogenic in the Norfolk fen country, where 'your onion crop sails over your head in a high wind' and your soil over the county border. Here, where the fertility build-up of centuries is claimed from the water by constant vigilance and an elaborate system of dykes and ditches, and is cashed in some of the biggest and best market garden crops, the only immediate necessity seems to be for nitrogen to enable other plant foods to be released from the soil. Although the debit balance already shows in the gradual subsidence of this rich soil, the only future check to production (and a consequent change in present management) would seem to be likely to occur when the level of this fabulous 'soot' ('muck land' to Americans) has receded to the point where telescopic ladders instead of garden paths will have to be attached to the front doors of houses!

There is still a lot of garden soil, even on market gardens, which is nothing but hungry, deep clay. Clay is normally rich in plant foods and produces fewer weeds than does a lighter soil, but no gardener would for choice start on such slowly improved land, some of which will devour enormous quantities of organic matter in the spring, yet revert to almost its original condition by the end of the season. For such clay, which is sticky and unworkable in wet weather (it should never be touched when in this putty-like state), cracked and hard as concrete when dry, cold and producing late-maturing crops, some of which do not over-winter well, treatment must be concentrated and long-term. In practice, one of two methods is used, involving minimum or maximum cultivation and soil disturbance.

The attraction of clay improvement and management by surface cultivation methods, particularly for the big waistline, the female and the labour-shy, is that after the first year this promises results without the expenditure of Herculean labour on repeated cultivations, the digging and 'working' of clay several times a year which is otherwise inevitable. Instead, labour is used to produce compost on a large scale, sufficient being needed to provide at least a layer 2 to 3 inches deep for that part of the garden under treatment. Surface cultivation, particularly of clay, will not work, nor will distinct improvement in texture show quickly, if much less compost than 20 tons to the acre is used to begin with. However, if such can be given, earlier planting dates, better crops and reduced labour for direct soil disturbance usually amply repay any additional cost.

The first step, which can't be avoided, is to bastard-trench (double-dig) clay when it is fairly dry during a dry spell in the autumn. This is in order to improve drainage mechanically, disrupt any pan and allow organic matter to be worked into the subsoil. Although the work is hard the method of bastard-trenching is simple. First, divide in two, lengthwise, the area to be trenched; then make a trench, 2 feet wide and 1 foot deep, half-way across the end of the plot, heaping the topsoil from this on to the path, for later filling into the last trench. Fork over thoroughly the subsoil at the bottom of the trench, working in some straw or other organic matter for drainage (do not use compost for this, as it would be wasted so far down). Then fill in the first trench with the topsoil from a second, dug side by side adjoining the first, at the same time mixing in decomposed organic matter, compost, peat, a little sand or rubble—in fact anything which will open the texture. Repeat this whole procedure until the end of the plot is reached, then cross over to the other side of the centre line and work in the reverse direction back to the starting end. By digging down one side and up the other, the last trench is made end to end with the first, the topsoil from which is then near to hand, does not have to be carried the full length of the plot as it otherwise would need to be if trenches were made the full width of the garden. Subsoiling of large gardens is an alternative to bastard-trenching. It should be done during a dry spell in summer or early autumn, when a good fracturing of the soil results and there is least chance of bringing useless subsoil to the surface. The essentials, of either method, are to avoid burying whatever good top soil there is, or bringing to the surface inert subsoil in which nothing will grow, and to add plenty of organic matter.

Compost, made of tough, fibrous materials (such as bracken and straw), especially if it is not fully mature, is one of the best texture-improvers. Peat, of the coarse $\frac{3}{8}-\frac{3}{4}$ inch grade, is also excellent, if well-wetted (it otherwise absorbs moisture from the surrounding soil) and dug in at the rate of a bucketful to the square yard. Such bulky organic manures are more economically and otherwise quite as successfully used as are the concentrated organic manures to improve clay, for the matters of chief importance are aeration, drainage and the supply of food for soil organisms, not the provision of large quantities of plant nutrients to ground which is normally rich in these. Thus, nitrogenous manures lacking much tough fibre give less value on clay than when used to activate compost-heaps, though farmyard manure with plenty of straw, bracken or peat litter, applied at the rate of 15 tons per acre, shows marked improvement of a heavy soil for some months, despite the fact that its use for such a purpose is somewhat wasteful in other respects.

Much clay is on the acid side. To raise the pH of acid clay, also to make it more friable and less sticky, lime (slaked lime on this occasion only; use otherwise ground chalk or limestone) should be applied during or after bastard-trenching, and in subsequent years thereafter for as long as the need for it is demonstrated by crops or weeds. Calcareous sea sand is a useful substitute for lime, so also is old mortar rubble. Ordinary sea or river sand, mixed with the clay, affects the pH but little, yet is useful in creating a more open texture. Wood ash, despite its usefulness as a neutralizer, should never be used on clay; it tends to make it excessively sticky and unmanageable.

Following bastard-trenching and the incorporation of organic matter (and while attention is focused on compost-making) the land under treatment should be left rough, to 'weather' (that is, for some of the large clods to break down) and to produce a weed crop. This growth should be lightly disced or cultivated under in the autumn (any lime requirement can be dealt with at the same time), and the land top-dressed with as much compost as can be provided. Undecomposed stuff will do, for it will decay during the following winter and will cause no nuisance in the spring. The more compost applied the better will be the result; 20 tons is not too much, but the main point is to try to have sufficient also for a further surface dressing the following spring. A mulch of really fine compost (first sieved if necessary), $\frac{1}{2}$ inch or more deep, creates the best sort of seed bed, if spread a few days before seeds or plants are to be set out. The roots of plants which are given a flying start in such a seed bed have enormous penetrating power; even swedes, turnips, carrots and parsnips fang but little when going down from compost into clay. (As a safeguard, stump-rooted varieties of some of these crops can be used, or the seeds be set in compost-filled dibble holes.)

In the autumn the bed should be cleared as usual of weeds and crop residues, and be lightly disturbed, but not inverted, to prevent caking and air insulation. A rotary cultivator will do the job very satisfactorily, as will an ordinary fork (with or without any special fulchrum attachment) shoved vertically into the ground at 6-inch intervals each way, worked about a bit and withdrawn. The annual mulch of compost—at least 2 inches thick, preferably more—should then be applied to the undug soil and topped with a little undecomposed organic material, such as sawdust or chaff if such is available. In the following spring it may be unnecessary to apply a dressing of fine compost to obtain a seed bed, for a light raking of the residue from the autumn mulch may give the sort of surface needed for regular and rapid germination of seedlings. However, maximum quantities of compost should be applied, as mulches during the growing season also, if best results are to be obtained.

Compost application, light soil disturbance (not inversion) and routine clearance of the bed, is the future treatment required by clay. Double-digging (or subsoiling) may be required only once every five or six years or not at all, as indicated by soil conditions and plant growth. Such soil disturbance sometimes proves to be altogether unnecessary, particularly in the garden run on the raised-bed system, or one on which a good rotation incorporating deep-rooting crops is employed. In almost all cases, satisfactory crops can be taken in the first year from the heaviest clay, with the minimum direct man-handling of the soil. The creation, by surface cultivation methods, of a new layer of topsoil (one of the aims of this treatment) is a slow process taking years, but its effect on crop yield and vigour, also subsequent ease of management, is sufficient reward for the effort needed. Those who are sceptical about the success of clay management by this method (which is equally successful in dealing with the subsoil problem) should try treating a small plot in this way, then repeat the treatment over the whole garden if, and when, it is proved to work more quickly or successfully than does a more orthodox method.

Sanctioned though it is by time-honoured custom, the system used by the gardener who persists in trying to cultivate away his clay is slow and back-breaking. More often than not the clay wins in the end, although only a trial will convince many a gardener of this. However, it works in some cases, and can be tried, if only for comparison to surface cultivation for the same purpose. It involves: bastard-trenching or subsoiling every second or third autumn; yearly deep-digging or ploughing in the autumn; the leaving of the soil rough-cultivated or ridged so as to expose the greatest possible area to the breaking-down effects of winter frosts; regular liming of the acid clays, usually those which contain much silt and, in addition, maximum cultivation during dry periods, with the incorporation of large quantities of organic matter. On occasions, top clay is burned, but this is a costly business, protracted and also unreliable, for no definite reaction to burning can be predicted; the clay is just as liable to set rock-hard, as it is to crumble down to a manageable texture (the aim of burning).

Those sandy loams which can be worked all the year round, including the time when clay is untouchable because too wet or dry, give the commercial gardener who makes most profit on early crops a head start over his heavy neighbour. However, all is not on the credit side for the cultivator of medium or light soil. The nearer soil gets to what is known as 'sandy soil' (over 90 per cent of sand), the large particles of which let water pass as through a cullander, taking soluble matter, nutrients and lime with it, the more skill is required of the gardener to avoid losing it altogether and to take from it three or four cash crops of good quality each year.

Continuous cropping and organic matter in ample supply are the main answers to the basic problems of light soil, namely moisture loss, leaching and blowing. Sandy soil is as free-draining in winter as in summer. Compost holds ten times its own weight of water against summer drought and supplies and encourages organisms which, directly or by means of metabolistic by-products, clamp together individual soil particles, thus creating a moisture-retentive soil of more stable structure. A rough compost is best for light soils in the first stage of improvement, for it is more retentive of moisture than is the fine variety. One which is rich in potash may be very useful in those districts, particularly the east of England sands, where deficiency of potash, a readily leached element, commonly occurs. Fortunately, seaweed and bracken, both of which are rich in potash, are usually available in bulk in such coastal areas. Maximum quantities of appropriate composts should be applied, preferably little and often as a mulch during the growing season, plus a general booster dressing of really heavy stuff each autumn. To place fine, mature compost into drills at seeding time in the spring is to give young plants best conditions for making rapid headway. Until successive years of organic

111

management have transformed very light land into something akin to the best medium loam, it should be kept always under a crop, if necessary a good stand of weeds, to reduce blowing and leaching to a minimum. Surface cultivation methods should not be tried until compost has been applied for three or four years, when the soil is really retentive of moisture.

The optimum pH reaction to be desired for sandy soils is between 6·0 and 6·5, and not above 7·0, but excessive acidity is sometimes caused, mainly by leaching of lime in drainage water. Annual applications of ground chalk or limestone at 2 oz. per square yard, or crushed organic shells if they can be obtained more easily, should therefore be made to such sands, until the time when high humus and organic matter content and earthworm casts maintain the soil's pH reaction where it is wanted: at its most favourable level for crops and soil organisms. A problem which may occur for the first year or so during organic cultivation, though it usually disappears later, is that of nitrogen shortage in early spring, when this element has been leached by winter rains or is locked up in early weed growth. An efficacious remedy, and not unnecessarily wasteful of valuable manure, is dried blood at the rate of 4 oz. per square yard, or a similar organic nitrogenous dressing, cultivated in a week to three weeks before seeds are set.

Similar treatment to that of light soils, minus the application of lime, is recommended for dealing with chalky soil (over 20 per cent of chalk or limestone). The necessity is mainly for organic matter in large quantities, some of the most useful functions of which on chalky soil are, preventing excessive drainage, eliminating characteristic stickiness in winter and wet weather, and acting as a buffer against excessive alkalinity. Excess of lime in the absence of organic matter means that potash, or other elements such as manganese, aluminium, zinc and copper, may be made unavailable to plants. Organic matter is the key to their release, but for the first year or so of organic cultivation on chalky soils which may be so deficient, to apply a compost rich in trace elements and potash (a job made easy by the help of seaweed) is an added help and safeguard against deficiency. The most urgent necessity is, however, to bring down the pH reaction of the very alkaline soil, the degree of which is reflected to the keen observer in the sickly yellowing of some plant leaves: lime-induced chlorosis. Coal ash will rapidly do the trick, but green manure, such as lawn mowings or leaf-mould, is safer; it has a similar acidifying effect, but milder, and is applied without the sulphur-risk.

Lack of lime is often a problem on otherwise fertile soil which shallowly overlays solid chalk but is separated from it, often by a hard pan. The need for surface liming is usually demonstrated by a generally heavy infestation of weeds, usually associated with acid soils. Treatment should consist of maximum compost application after disruption of any pan by bastard-trenching or subsoiling, and the use of deep-rooting plants in the rotation to help base exchange between lower and upper soil levels. The very unconsolidated chalks, which puff up like meringues during frosty weather, also pay for rolling in spring, which helps to create a more suitable structure for rooting and helps to tide plants over drought periods—thus serving the same purpose as once did trampling sheep, driven over farm lands on England's limestone hills and chalky downs. Surface cultivation methods do well on chalky soils in areas of average rainfall.

Compost provides, in a single parcel, not only an all-purpose fertilizer but also the only really satisfactory soil conditioner: humus, the relatively stable substance left after fungi and bacteria have just about finished with organic matter as a source of food. Humus, with the help of organic matter in all stages of decay, does very effectively the job of maintaining most garden soils in a suitable physical condition, provided that it is continually replenished; sufficient is provided by the ordinary compost heap, particularly that which contains woody material such as sawdust, shavings or thick prunings. Except in extreme cases, such as the rapid improvement of very heavy clay not previously organically managed, there is never the slightest need by the organic gardener to buy in peat or the now familiar synthetic soil conditioners, merely to improve the structure of his soil or to stop this from blowing.

Bad as conditions are in some orthodox gardens, very little garden soil in Britain could benefit from the addition of high-priced synthetic substitutes for natural humus components, the so-called soil conditioners, a sort of heart massage for soils at death's door. About a dozen such conditioners are now on the market, some as compounds containing also inorganic or organic fertilizers. The conditioner constituent is simply any one of the many substances which could be synthesized, to hold moisture, for example, and could do more harm than good on any soil other than an exhausted one, or in a dust-bowl. Fearful might be the consequences of making clay a hundred times more moisture-retaining than by digging in peat; of applying a conditioner to certain British gardens in our climate, or of applying it at the wrong time (certain of the conditioners 'freeze' or stabilize a soil, in whatever condition such a soil is when the conditioner is applied; they do not change a sandy soil into a medium loam—as compost will do). They cannot replace humus.

ORGANIC CULTIVATION

Where the present-day 'orthodox' gardener is organically biased but makes use, too, of chemical fertilizers, weed killers and objectionable pesticides, the all-organic enthusiast relies entirely on garden compost to create a healthy soil able to sustain healthy, health-giving plant life. Unlike chemical fertilizers which are noted for their rapid action and which supply nutrients to plants more or less directly, the action of garden compost is slower and its beneficial action may not be apparent for some weeks or months. In the long term the continued use of garden compost creates a 'fertility bank' in the soil with the soil itself also transformed beneficially.

For the gardener, the commercial man or members of a commune wishing to go all-organic there is usually a transition period between the time when the decision has been made to change from partial organic methods to a complete change-over to all-organic husbandry. This transition period may be a matter of months or a matter of a few years depending on the treatment the soil has received previously. In a small back garden where either some garden compost may have been used or none at all, the soil may be simply 'hungry'. To soils of this sort heavy applications of garden compost lead rapidly to a beneficial action on soil structure and plant growth. Results are particularly striking with summer cabbages, potatoes and tomatoes. It is where chemical fertilizers and other chemical potions have been used regularly that one comes up against soil sickness. This may be due to pollution by insoluble chemical residues or to an unbalance caused by excessive applications of lime to counteract acidity caused by chemical fertilizers. Sick soils may be devoid of large fungal, bacterial and insect populations such as is the norm in a biologically sound soil. If garden compost and this only is used in one fell swoop with the simultaneous discontinuation of pest controls, the gardener may well be disappointed at his early results with all-organic methods. Time must be allowed for the soil to become de-polluted, as it were, and for patience on the part of the gardener during the transition period needed by an unbalanced soil to right itself and rid itself of pollutants. Just how long a soil will take to rejuvenate itself depends on the original sick condition which needs righting. Three years is sometimes quoted as the minimum. During the change-over to all-organic gardening no chemical fertilizers should be used. Weed killers should also be omitted from the programme and although it may be necessary to use pesticides these should be non-toxic to man, household pets and wildlife. Derris and pyrethrum are typical of this class of pesticide. Sulphur is a traditional non-poisonous mildew repellent.

Five or six years may be needed to rejuvenate the much polluted soils of some large commercial establishments where chemicalized methods have been practised for so long that many poisonous residues in the soil impede the natural break down of organic matter added to it in the form of garden compost. In such establishments where the profit motive is uppermost, chemicalized methods may have to be continued for some time but their use should be on a greatly diminished scale and with very heavy compost applications made as often as possible. Where appropriate, the pest control measures outlined in Chapter VI should be used.

Not all pests and diseases may disappear by the time it is decided that the transition period is at an end and that from then on the holding will be run on an all-organic basis. However, most will. Those troubles which continue will not cause great losses to crops. Their ravages will be controlled effectively by ladybirds and the many other allies which those who garden organically have.

The advantages of organic gardening methods are so real that there is no known occasion on record of anyone having changed back to chemicalized gardening after having given organic methods a trial. The better the quality of the prepared garden compost, the better the organic gardener's success is likely to be. Little better than useless is a heap of unfermented rubbish which passes on disease organisms and weed seeds to the soil and is also wet and smelly. Applications of well-made garden compost should, where possible, be made generously and not sprinkled around the garden like sugar on a pie. Garden compost is a complete manure—not a quick-acting fertilizer.

An April-made heap will provide garden compost for use as a thick mulch in which June-planted seedlings may be set. Late summer wastes link up with the autumn clean-up in the garden. A heap completed and covered by Guy Fawkes Day decomposes slowly during

115

winter and is ready for use in March and April. An autumn-made heap is of especial use around Easter at potato-planting time. If sieved, compost from an autumn-made heap can be used as a propagating medium in trays and pots when seed sowing starts in April. Sieved garden compost is also an excellent top dressing for seed beds whether in the open, in frames or beneath cloches. The fortunate gardener who has a compost heap ready for use in the autumn may protect his soil from frosts and heavy rain damage and encourage maximum activity by earthworms and other soil life in winter by mulching the ground with compost in late October or early November. Compost applied then should preferably be rough and not fully decomposed. If this compost mulch can be topped off with some sawdust or chaff—so much the better.

If garden compost is applied regularly and generously then the use of organically based fertilizers is never necessary. To the beginner in organic gardening it would possibly seem desirable to provide a table of compost requirements for particular crops. But such a table would encourage in the beginner an idea that it is his plants rather than his soil and its vast population which he is feeding. This would shift the emphasis of the production of healthy, health-giving whole-food in a healthy soil to a plant fertilizer basis. All organic theories and practices are based on the principle that a healthy soil is the prime requisite for the production of good, healthy food crops. However, after a soil has been rejuvenated, is 'clean' and biologically alive, it is right to bear in mind that when compost—and there is never enough of it in most gardens—is being applied some crops are noted gross feeders. Tomatoes, potatoes and cauliflowers come to mind. These subjects will benefit most from heavier dressings of garden compost than will, say, carrots, lettuce and radish.

Although, as has been stated several times already, the all-organic gardener relies entirely for soil health, soil fertility and healthy plant growth on garden compost there may well be insufficient compost at first to apply to the total garden area. Understandably, the gardener will not wish parts of the garden to remain uncultivated whilst waiting for sufficient compost. It is at such an occasion as this when organic 'aids' such as composts prepared from fruit pulp, fish wastes or horse manure can be of value. It is very necessary for the gardener to appreciate that these organic mixtures do not have the same high rating as has garden compost. They also have to be paid for and their cost increases the price of home-grown food crops.

CHAPTER VI

SOME EXAMPLES OF ORGANIC CONTROL
OF PESTS AND DISEASES

It is the belief of every organic gardener that a healthy soil is conducive to the healthy growth of plants, and animals and humans fed on those plants. Diseases and pests are considered as mainly symptomatic of pathological soil conditions or indicative of biological unbalance.

Experience teaches that, in time, balance between pests and predators, and an amazing degree of disease resistance, can be built up on the organic garden. Many troubles vanish of their own accord, as it were, and every experienced composter is able to quote an impressive number of those prevented or controlled without the aid of any special measures such as are used by the orthodox gardener. As yet, however, it has not proved possible, simply by applying compost and otherwise employing efficient organic methods, to keep off all the time all the pests and diseases which arise from our need to grow plants together in larger quantities than would occur in nature. For example, the health of a compost-grown crop may not repel locusts, or the Colorado beetle, which under natural conditions was a pest of the American plant species allied to our Woody and Deadly Nightshades. What we can do is to assist nature to keep pests and diseases to manageable proportions, so that, instead of being a constant problem, they are merely occasional misfortunes. We co-operate on the principle that prevention is better than cure and allow nature the first crack at offenders. Then, if necessary, we attack with weapons which, in the main, are specially selected for their innocuousness in all respects other than the purpose for which they are used. (This cannot be said of the poisons and sprays used by the orthodox, the effects of which, other than those intended, are in many cases seriously harmful.)

ORGANIC CONTROL OF PESTS AND DISEASES

The health of crops on the truly organic garden of many years standing is no mere figment of the imagination. This would be true, even were three-quarters of the reports of 'complete health' grossly exaggerated, or the supposedly beneficial effects of organic methods were in actual fact attributable to causes such as the non-recognition of viruses and other troubles (a frequent fault of most amateur gardeners). Of the many who have recorded in thousands of different parts of the world that very real qualities of immunity to disease and pest attack are conferred by organic cultivation, all cannot be wrong. Those who think otherwise need only give organic methods a thorough trial. In view of this it is a pity that so little is known about the mechanism of plant resistance or immunity, and the maintenance of positive health. However, the organic gardener observes in practice the advantages conferred by his system of cultivation, the logic of which is easily seen.

Plants grown in fertile soil, well supplied with organic matter, receive adequate and constant supplies of minerals and inorganic nutrients; they are therefore less likely to suffer from deficiency diseases, also some 'secondary' diseases connected with deficiency, than are plants not so grown. They also benefit from the presence of antibiotics, also other growth-promoting and health-fostering substances and organisms (contributed by the compost heap and manufactured or encouraged in the soil). Some of these, it has been suggested, may make changes in the cell structure of plants or make their sap unattractive to certain pests. Due to the presence of soil fungi, such as certain species of mycorrhiza, such difficult subjects as conifers and (tip-cuttings of) Ericas are enabled to 'take' and thrive well in organically managed soil. Compost-grown plants are also much less liable to suffer from physiological disorders, for they are raised under a system, one of the main effects of which is the maintenance of maximum health in a soil of good structure and physical condition. Of course, it goes without saying that the application of compost alone will not confer, as so many beginners fondly imagine, immunity from (although it may minimize) the effects of poor cultivations or aeration, bad drainage, overcrowding of crops or the growing of unsuitable varieties.

Of the part which biological control or balance plays, both in and about the soil, many illustrations could be given. The following estimate was made in 1933 by J. E. Moss. Of 10,000 caterpillars (large Cabbage White Butterfly) hatched, 59·17 per cent are destroyed by disease; of the 4,083 remaining, 84·21 per cent are destroyed by *Apanteles* (parasites); of the 645 left, 27·0 per cent are destroyed by disease as pupae; of the 471 left, 3·0 per cent are destroyed by *Pteromalus* as pupae; of the 457 left, 93 per cent are destroyed by birds, leaving 32 to complete the life cycle.

Of the many species of soil-inhabiting predatory nematodes, at least 25-odd species are capable of capturing and consuming eel-worms and other soil animals. They have been found in far greater numbers in compost, than in decaying vegetation, and in composted than uncomposted soil, and there is reason to believe that it is through their agency that it is possible, as so many growers have dis-covered, to clean up in one year or two years a bad infestation of potato eelworm by the application of compost alone. Finally, every organic gardener has observed, or been told, how a few ladybirds have disposed of an entire colony of aphides in a matter of hours or days.

The organic gardener maintains this balance and obtains its bene-fits whereas the orthodox cultivator frequently upsets it, by applying a virulent poison or by sterilizing his soil. In the opinion of the for-mer, the latter's game is not worth the candle. For example, DDT (at one time almost accepted by orthodox gardeners as the answer to every pest but now frowned upon by all knowledgeable folk and its use banned in some countries) is ineffective against Red Spider Mite, yet kills its natural predators and enemies and can result in a rapid increase of this pest. Far more poison residue falls beneath the sprayed orchard tree, than is collected on its branches, foliage or flowers, and may seriously affect beneficial soil organisms. Sterilization eliminates tem-porarily both beneficial and disease-producing organisms, earthworms and all other soil inhabitants. Apart from all these immediate effects, there is the questionable 'beneficial' effect on soil, plant, animal and human health, of the continued absorption of residues of those poisons normally used to control pests and disease. There is a 'maximum residue' permitted by statute, but does any orthodox grower bother to see that this is not exceeded on his produce?

The organic gardener interferes as little as possible with the im-mensely complex balance between pests and predators, a balance which, strange as it may seem, is usually in his favour, except when epidemics occur. A sound knowledge of the principles and techniques he applies, and a realization that nature may not be chivvied, are his effective insurances against most troubles, provided that his 'policy' is taken out immediately he commences to change over from orthodox to organic methods.

Where a soil is not completely healthy there can be some troubles from pests and diseases during the transition period when the gardener or commercial man is doing his best to rejuvenate his land. The first step in the control of common pests and diseases is, therefore, gradually to wean the garden from orthodox (organic + chemical) to all-organic methods, for which, as already stated a minimum period of three years is sometimes needed. At the end of this time, and more so as time passes, plants can to a great extent withstand or grow away from attack, or are protected by a police force of beneficial organisms exercising constant vigilance against the garden's spivs and underworld. During and after conversion, traffic control of diseased plants or vegetation should, of course, be in the direction of the compost heap, the Old Bailey of the organic garden. The totally unnatural degree of heating (achieved by natural means during the composting process) enables most, if not all, of the disease-producers imported on infected material to be killed. The experienced composter need not hesitate to put infected material into his heap, for 'baking and bugs' will render it into a clean and valuable plant food. (Pathogens do not usually breed in compost heaps.) Maximum control is achieved for a little extra trouble in seeing that the composting process is thorough.

Of the many weapons (other than composting, that is) which the gardener uses to discourage offenders, several automatically become a part of organic cultivation. Examples are, plant rotation and the growing of crop varieties suited to a particular area and soil type, also the choosing of varieties resistant or immune to particular pests or diseases which have been proved, by experience, to be especially troublesome in a particular locality. One of the most important 'remedies' in this category is the raising of (most) crops from compost -grown seeds or plants, preferably home-grown or saved, otherwise purchased. Better plants of most species are produced if raised from seed suited and adapted to their environment by years of 'ancestral residence'.

The remainder of this chapter is mainly comprised of suggestions, and suggested weapons, to help in the banishment from the organic garden of some pests and diseases which may remain as a legacy of previous orthodoxy, those which are particularly persistent for some reason or another, or those which occur as epidemics. In parts it is merely a plea for no special treatment to be given, but an explanation or illustration of how biological or 'natural' control functions, or hints for the raising of particular crops with increased resistance in view. It is in no respect the equivalent of a complicated spraying programme. The methods recommended, some of which, admittedly, are archaic and time-occupying, have all been proved to be effective in many cases or, if there is doubt that they may work, it is expressed. To give an 'organic gardening doctor' is to stick one's neck out, and hits at the supply of poisons and fumigants which fill the advertising columns of the gardening press. The writer has kept in mind that, it is no use quoting as 'gospel', some remedy-recommendation which someone has tried once in a year when there has been no infection for miles around.

The organic gardener will need this chapter when he begins, but should need it less and less as time goes on and he gains more experience. It is during the final change-over period, and for a few years after it, that he will find it most useful. To know all the control measures for a particular trouble is to be able to choose that which will be most suitable all round.

Not all pests and diseases are dealt with in this chapter, which could usefully be expanded to a hundred times its present length. Special control measures are not needed for many pests and diseases which are common elsewhere than on the organic garden, and others to deal with yet other troubles still remain to be evolved or recorded. The Henry Doubleday Research Association is keenly interested in this aspect of organic gardening and has published many helpful booklets including *Pest Control without Poisons*, price 20p (post free).

Bats, hedgehogs, frogs and toads are nice to have about and do valuable work. There is no way of encouraging bats but hedgehogs stay in or near the garden where the thoughtful owner puts out a saucer of milk of a summer evening and a frog or toad colony can be established if there is a garden pool—without fishes in it. A temporary pool in which frogs and toads can breed each spring may be constructed easily and cheaply with 500-gauge blue or black polythene sheeting. The sheeting should be used doubled and laid on a pad of sifted sand, sifted ash, peat or wads of damp newspapers.

The organic gardener should encourage all carnivorous beetles and unpaid assistant pest destroyers. The centipede, the red-brown creature, eats many small-scale plant enemies. The millipede, much more slender, with more legs and yellow in colour, eats mainly rotten wood and vegetable matter so is not as useful. The large violet ground beetle and the Devil's Coach Horse are greedier and more valuable still. Avoiding poison sprays means an increase in natural predators, but those who squash recklessly when these creatures become common are protecting the pests.

An example of this took place at Kew during the war. By 1939 the rock garden had a large population of carnivorous slugs, big, black, and with horns like a cat's ears, carefully introduced and making an impression on the common slug population. When the introducer was away on war service, Land Army and other weeders collected the hard-working carnivores with the alpine-eating enemy and destroyed both. This action led to an increased population of harmful common slugs.

The virtues of earthworms are well known, and by creating best conditions for their survival and breeding (as, indeed, the composter does), we can encourage the large numbers which go a long way to manuring and draining our land. The point to remember about earthworms is, that if they are absent from your soil there is usually a reason for it, for example, scarcity of organic matter, the use of sulphate of ammonia or other inorganics in heavy dosage, the airlessness and impermeability of clay, or the lack of moisture (as in certain American states). They can be a paying proposition for the man who 'worm farms' by the methods recommended by T. H. Barrett (*Harnessing the Earthworm*, Faber), but it is a waste of money to buy and add them to a soil which is not well supplied with organic matter, their principal food, or to soil which is unsuited to them for some other reason. The man who makes compost usually gets earthworms by the million.

APHIDES (*Aphididae*) (greenfly, blackfly, plant lice, etc.)

A great many plants, grown under orthodox conditions, appear to be susceptible to one or other of the 200-odd species of aphis. Many of these same plants, grown on an organic garden, appear to have much more resistance to attack, or are adequately protected through biological agencies. E. B. Balfour, in *The Living Soil* (Faber), confirms many other writers by saying: 'My own experience extending over several seasons has convinced me that crops of the cabbage family, if grown from seedlings raised on humus-rich soil and transplanted on to land treated with compost, show markedly greater resistance to caterpillar and aphis attack than those grown with artificials *or even with ordinary farmyard manure.* . . . I have noticed that both compost and chemically grown plants will be attacked, but whereas the plants grown with chemicals (if left unprotected) will in a bad season, be stripped to the rib, those grown with compost (with the exception of the isolated plant) are only slightly damaged and recover quickly.' (My italics—author.) Partial or complete immunity has been observed by the writer and recorded by many others, to most aphid species, of a wide range of plants. The late Sir Albert Howard remarked that Woolly Aphis (see below) was the last pest to leave his converted Blackheath garden, after three years of compost treatment and *without active measures of pest control having been used.*

For the organic gardener, the ladybird and her grub, the grubs of the Brown Lacewing (*Boriomya subnebulosa*), hymenopterous wasps and bugs of the *Anthorocid* species, frequently demonstrate the effectiveness of biological control, for often an infestation of greenfly, occurring in a bad season, is found to be entirely cleaned up in a matter of hours or days. Numbers of these predators and parasites, if not deterred by orthodox spray treatments, increase rapidly and form a healthy plant's greatest insurance against future attack. Sound nutrition further enables susceptible plants to grow away from attack and suffer negligible damage. Complementary to biological control and the health of the plant, are high standards of cultivation and ordinary garden hygiene. New plants should be inspected for cleanliness; the grower should also remove alternative weed hosts (such as Yarrow (*Achillea millefolium*), Groundsel (*Senecio* spp.), the *Umbelliferae*, etc.), especially near glasshouses. He should adequately space crops so that there is no overcrowding, that frequent fault of the amateur. Space presents some barrier to the wingless, viviparous female aphides, even though wind or ants may bridge the gaps between plants.

Dramatic reduction of aphis numbers cannot be expected before the end of the conversion to organics or during the first few all-organic seasons. For this reason, derris (the relatively harmless powder or liquid) should be one of the last orthodox munitions against this pest to be abandoned, and a tin should be kept handy on a shelf, but not used unnecessarily. In the small garden, and if a stirrup pump or spray which gives good hitting force is available, a solution of 2 oz. of soft soap to a gallon of water can with advantage replace derris, except for soaking lettuce transplants if an infestation is really bad. To plant broad beans, one of the more seriously affected crops, as early as possible in the year, and to nip out the fully grown tips (the favourite tender growth), also to remove affected leaves, helps to prevent attack and extend control. A fortune awaits the gardener who can suggest a method of getting and keeping rid of all the species of aphis, quick, complete, sure, and more important, completely innocuous in other respects.

To combat Woolly Aphis on apple trees, a remedy was originally recommended by the late Dr. Rudolf Steiner, and elaborated by others. This is to paint or spray affected trees with a distillation or extract of nasturtiums, and to broadcast these (self-seeding) flowers under the trees as a permanent control. It is suggested that an aromatic substance, repellent in smell or taste to the Woolly Aphis, is absorbed into the sap by the tree roots. The author has tried this (without the spray) with three badly infested apple trees, one left as a control in each year, the ground below the other two seeded from a small packet of colourful nasturtiums. There was no sign (and has been none since) of Woolly Aphis on the treated trees. A considerable infestation occurred on the untreated control, in the first two years, but this tree, also, became 'clean' and for the past three years has needed no further attention in this respect. 'Twelve-tree orchardists' may like to try this measure, which involves no effort or trouble apart from initial distribution of seed, or to adopt another efficient control: that of rubbing a little vaseline over the easily seen colonies of the aphis and of protecting, by the same method, abrasions or pruned stumps which are the parts of the tree most likely to be attacked. The nasturtiums can be trained up strings into the branches or tied against the trunk, they will flower even in the shade of the leaves though not so well as in the open, they can do no harm and are decorative even in the garden of the most sceptical.

A remedy which has proved very effective in practice, both in the large commercial orchard and the small one, is to introduce the parasite of the Woolly Aphis. Eggs of the parasite, *Aphelinus mali*, are collected on small bundles of twigs which are then suspended on affected trees. There appears to be no source of supply of these eggs in Britain at the present time (1975).

The 'organic world' is at the present time taking great interest in the use of garlic as a deterrent to aphis. Research work in the United States has already shown that garlic sprays are of use in combating

ORGANIC CONTROL OF PESTS AND DISEASES

some mildews and bacteria. That members of the onion family are of use in controlling aphis is not something quite new. Several organic gardeners are quite sure that chives planted around their peach trees and rose bushes prevent aphis damage.

BIG BUD MITE (Blackcurrant Gall Mite)

Minute grey mites which cause buds on blackcurrant bushes to swell. The abnormal buds are very noticeable in spring when leaves do not appear from the buds which wither. On redcurrant and white currant bushes the buds simply die instead of first swelling. Gooseberry bushes may be attacked but this is rare. On gooseberries the symptoms are as on redcurrants. Big Bud can reduce crops drastically and if an infestation is not controlled the only solution is to grub up the bushes. Infected buds should be picked off in September and March and then burnt. Spraying with lime sulphur or with other chemicals is an orthodox answer to this pest. But such sprays can kill the natural predator of the mites, *Anthocoris nemorum*. The organic gardener is never eager to use chemical products and experience shows that organic methods, particularly where they involve no disturbance to bush roots but with the application of heavy mulches of compost, can (coupled with hand-picking of affected buds) deal with this trouble.

CABBAGE WHITE BUTTERFLIES

These pests lay eggs on the foliage of brassicas. Caterpillars hatch and can strip the plants leaving them looking like ancient hulks at low tide. Many organic gardeners report that although they observe these unpleasant caterpillars contentedly gnawing cabbage foliage yet the damage is minimal. It is not really understood as yet why it is that brassicas growing in an organically-rich soil and receiving sufficient moisture are seldom plagued with cabbage caterpillars. One theory is that because the cabbages are 'whole-food' the caterpillars need far less foliage for their growth and organically-grown brassicas therefore suffer far less damage than do similar plants growing in soil which itself is not in the best of health. Another theory is also based on the good health of the soil idea. It is thought that cabbage white butterflies are natural scavengers. Their job is to sort out the sheep from the goats. The butterflies are therefore guided to less healthy plants—which is to say plants not growing in healthy soil. That cabbage white butterflies are often seen in vast quantities is the fault of man himself. By planting vast acreages of cabbages, cauliflowers, broccoli and kale, the butterflies have no need to seek plants in the wild. Man supplies more than enough plants for egg laying. Even in the organic garden or holding, complete immunity from caterpillar damage is rare but that it can occur is demonstrated below.

H. R. Massy records, in the autumn 1950 issue of *Mother Earth*, his experiences with 6 acres of kale, manured with immature compost at the rate of about 20 tons to the acre, in an area where considerable damage from caterpillar attack was reported in that year. Thousands of white butterflies had been observed over the field in question for several days, but a decision to dust was rescinded (after DDT had been purchased) when yard by yard examination of about an acre of the field revealed that, although butterflies were settling on the kale, none or few appeared to be depositing eggs. Indeed, only two agglomerates of eggs were found. All the butterflies departed within twenty four hours or thereabouts, and Massy records that no damage at all was discovered subsequently.

Resistance of this degree may not always be built up until well after the conversion period, during which, therefore, derris is best kept in the garden shed in case it is needed. An important control measure in the small garden is to hand-pick and destroy egg clusters, green caterpillars, chrysalids over-wintering in soil or crevices, and to catch the white butterflies. Most children love to co-operate! Give the caterpillars no time to grow, for they eat voraciously. Thorough drenching of plants (the under- as well as upper-surfaces of their leaves), with 2 oz. of common salt dissolved in a gallon of water, is an effective control measure, most useful on the small garden.

Bear in mind that in your fight against cabbage white caterpillars you have a very efficient natural killer. This is the ichneumon wasp, sometimes called 'ichneumon fly'. Eggs of some ichneumons are laid inside caterpillars. The grubs hatch and devour the living host. Ichneumons which parasitize caterpillars of cabbage whites emerge from the dead caterpillars and spin very small cocoons. These resemble silkworm cocoons being oval and pale yellow in colour. The cocoons are usually in small batches on the foliage of brassicas. Learn to recognize these cocoons. The more friendly (to you but not to cabbage whites) ichneumons you have in the garden the less fear you may have of badly gnawed cabbages.

CLUBROOT (Finger-and-Toe)

Recognition of this worst fungus disease of the brassicae and cruci-ferae is often found difficult by the amateur, to whom the best advice that can be given is, make sure your plants have really got it before adopting control measures. Symptoms of this disease as displayed in foliage are at times very much like those of severe drought, and damage depends to a great extent on the stage at which plants are attacked. Young plants make anaemic, stunted growth; if cabbages and cauli-flowers, they rarely heart and often die. Plants attacked during middle-age often turn yellow, also wilt, especially in the heat of day during hot, dry periods, and their outer leaves die. Foliage symptoms alone are not enough for diagnosis of club-root, confirmation of which must depend mainly on evidence supplied by the root system of the affected plant. Even then, the 'hernias' or 'tumours' of club-root are often confused with the galls produced by the Turnip Gall Weevil. This is a common but much less serious pest which, when it leaves the root, leaves a hole—by means of which the offender can be identified. Occasionally club-root is confused with completely innocuous 'hybridization nodules' on some plant species (which, however, do not smell or decay prematurely, as do club-root-infected roots). Where *Plasmodiophora* has gained a good foothold, there is usually agonized distortion of some roots, which may be anything up to ten times their normal diameter, encrusted with characteristic swellings, spherical, spindle-shaped or merely irregular. Usually, there is also scabbiness, but the infallible symptom is a mottled or marbled cross-section of the affected root. Sometimes new roots are present above the seat of infection.

If affected plants are left in the soil, their enlarged root cells soften and decay into a stinking, semi-liquid mass and release millions of spores which, under certain conditions, rest in the soil until another susceptible crop is grown. These quiescent spores do not multiply in the absence of a host plant. Theoretically, they can be starved out of land which can be left unused by any susceptible crop for seven or eight years, if no host plants, such as Charlock, Wild Mustard, or Shepherd's Purse, exist as weeds. However, this control measure is rarely adopted, for it means the absence of many plants which usually find their way on to the table at least once a day, and the causative fungus can be only too easily introduced or transported on seeds, seedlings, boots, machinery, also in the dung of animals which have consumed affected roots. (This last mode of entry is one of the reasons why it is wise to avoid the use of untreated animal manures on a club-rooted patch of ground.)

The writer has heard of no case in which club-root has persisted in serious proportions for more than one year after infected land has been adequately treated with compost, and appropriate precautions have been taken against the spread of the disease in such ways as the failure to destroy or properly compost diseased roots. The killing temperatures reached in the heap and microbial antagonisms which continue when compost is applied to the soil, seem to be extremely efficient in clearing up an infestation, given the maintenance of ordinary garden hygiene. This involves getting up infected plants before their roots decay, by carefully digging them out with some surrounding soil, transporting them to the composting site, cutting off edible portions there, and composting the remainder by the method recommended in Chapter IV. A good composting method is less wasteful than the burning of club-rooted plants, and is safer than feeding them to animals which may pass viable organisms in their dung. As much compost as possible should be applied to the club-rooted infected land. Give a heavy dressing in the autumn and fill trenches or dibble holes which are to take transplants. Club-root is more liable to develop to really serious proportions (mainly on the orthodox garden) in an acid soil, so apply ground chalk or limestone at the rate of 4 oz. per square yard for a year or two after infection has occurred without bothering to take a soil analysis. Remove susceptible weeds, and do not grow susceptible crops (or mustard for green manure) on the infected ground for as long as possible. The courageous sometimes follow suitable compost treatment by growing such crops as cabbages and swedes, but for experimental purposes only. An obvious precaution is to give them the go-by for as long as possible by employing a suitable rotation of crops.

COMMON SCAB OF POTATOES

Efficient methods of making compost and its generous application, the turning-in of green manure crops (to increase acidity as well as fertility), and the selection of resistant varieties of potato, seem to be the only special control measures which the organic gardener can use

ORGANIC CONTROL OF PESTS AND DISEASES

against potato scab, when, during conversion, he abandons the orthodox organo-mercury dips, formaldehyde or mercuric chloride.

EELWORM

There are many species of eelworm, of which the following are but
a few: *Heterodera marioni* (the 'Root Knot Eelworm') is indiscrimin-
ately parasitic, but is particularly troublesome on tomatoes and
cucumbers; *H. rostochiensis* (the 'Potato Root Eelworm') parasitizes
potatoes, tomatoes, Woody Nightshade and other plants of the Sele-
nacae; *Aphelenchoides ritzema-bosi* (the 'Chrysanthemum Eelworm')
attacks chrysanthemums, tomatoes, etc.; *Anguillulina dipsaci* (the
'Stem and Bulb Eelworm'), is found on tomatoes and clover.

Most, if not all, species of eelworm known to be harmful to crops
have been found to be discouraged by organic cultivation. Two
reports of the many recorded by organic growers in all parts of the
world, will serve to illustrate the present position.

E. B. Balfour, in a letter to *The Times*, of Monday, 12th September
1949, states: 'On a nursery at Wisbech eight consecutive crops of
white iris have been grown under glass in the same soil without
sterilization, with no pest control treatment and no fertilization other
than an annual dressing of organic compost. Two years ago the
species of eelworm known to attack this crop was deliberately introduced into this house, but so far no sign of damage has resulted.'

P. H. Hainsworth writes, in *The Grower*, Vol. 40, No. 11, of
12th September 1953: 'A small plot (of potatoes), deliberately infected with eelworm two years ago was divided into halves—one
half dug and manured with potato fertilizer at 10 cwt. an acre and the
other undug, but the top 3 inches loosened sufficiently to draw up a
ridge. This was manured with organically activated compost at 30
tons per acre. Eelworm samples taken by the N.A.A.S. shortly before
the tops died off showed six times as many cysts in the artificial plot.
The potatoes dug recently showed a 50 per cent increase in favour of
the compost plot.'

It should be noted that elimination or control of eelworm is the
usual aim! These (and other) accounts of courageous composting
experiments are particularly telling because, in each case, a valuable
crop has been 'jeopardized' by the deliberate introduction to a commercial nursery and a market garden of one of their worst pests.
Similar reports to the above cover the experiences of a government

129

agriculturist dealing with tobacco eelworm in Southern Rhodesia and many other examples of successful control or eradication. There are also endless enthusiastic (though poorly documented) reports in letters from amateurs, all of which go to prove that most species of eelworm (minute, transparent nematodes, which can enter plant tissue from the thin film of moisture surrounding its foliage, as well as from the soil via its roots) are prevented from establishing themselves or can be quickly controlled, on the organic garden. This success is achieved, in most cases, by compost treatment only, not by the application of any special control measures. Compost supplies not only adequate organic matter, which does much to ensure faultless nutrition of plants, but also an invisible police force of vast numbers of predatory fungi, some twenty-five species of which, including *Arthrobotrys musiformis* and *Dactylella lysipaga*, have been found to attack and consume eelworms. E. B. Balfour in *The Living Soil*, (Faber, p. 121) describes the methods employed by the predatory fungi to do this. 'The majority of the nematode-eating species form loops or bales of mycelium which also usually excrete an adhesive substance. When an eelworm crawls through these bales, they close round it, holding it captive despite its violent struggles which may last for as long as two and a half hours. When the captive becomes inert, the fungus bores through the skin of its prey, making a narrow penetration. A globous body is then formed by the penetrating mycelium, which increases in size until in an hour or two it has filled a transverse section through the animal's body. Lateral elongated branches then grow from this, passing between the captive's internal organs, until they fill its entire length. This causes paralysis and death of the eelworm, after which the fungus consumes all the internal fatty material of its body, leaving the cuticle untouched.'

These predatory fungi are normally found in decaying vegetation, in animal manures, and *in very large numbers* in organic compost. Their antagonistic operations are started in the heap and continue when compost is applied to the soil. Apart from this, there is also the direct effect of the destruction of eelworm at the high temperatures reached during the composting process, which enables infected plant tissue to be reduced to clean plant foods with complete safety.

Faultless nutrition as a result of compost fertilization undoubtedly has some effect on the resistance of crops to eelworm, particularly in the case of potatoes and tomatoes, also chrysanthemums (of which not only the roots, but stems, leaves and even flower tissue may be invaded). This strength is an invisible asset the value of which can only be measured over the years.

FLEA-BEETLES

Phyllotreta nemorum (the Turnip Flea-Beetle) and *P. vittata* (the Cabbage Flea-Beetle) appear to be two of the most persistent pests on organic gardens in some areas, despite the fact that there are many enthusiastic reports of their absence or reduction in others. During the first year or so after conversion to organic methods it may be necessary to dust seedlings of susceptible subjects with derris. This should be applied as soon as the seedlings show themselves and then at weekly intervals until the first true leaves figure on the seedlings. Do not use proprietary chemical flea-beetle dusts. Incidence of attack is, in the writer's opinion, much tied up with the methods and quality of organic management employed.

Susceptible plants are: broccoli, cabbages, kale, swedes, turnips, etc. Attack is shown by 'pin-head' or 'shot-holes' made by the adult beetles in cotyledons and leaves at the 'pre-rough' stage of growth, and larvae-attacked stems or root tissue. The organic gardener's main insurance against such attack is the encouragement of early, quick and regular plant growth.

Methods of cultivation can help to buttress these initial advantages. To lightly roll sandy soils in which seed has been sown favours moisture-retention and removes the cracks which can be convenient hiding-places in this serious game of hide-and-seek. To keep hedges, ditches, and the garden free of rubbish and large clods where these pests might pass the winter, and to eliminate charlock and weeds of the Preshaugh family (alternative hosts), is to provide fewest chances of survival. Cloche-grown crops are given added protection by glass and because of earlier planting dates.

ONION-FLY

E. B. Balfour, in *The Living Soil* (Faber), p. 125, observes that she has 'grown onions in a soil rich in humus which produced an abundantly healthy crop in a season when practically the whole onion crop of the surrounding district was destroyed by onion-fly'. Such experience has also been that of many other organic growers, most of whom stress the importance of growing susceptible onions, leeks and shallots in a four-course, or similar, rotation and the generous use of compost, which encourages rapid and healthy growth of young plants in spring when they are prone to be attacked. The best advice that can be given is to sow early, or in autumn, on well-composted land, in order to get healthy, hard bulbs by the time the onion-fly is on the wing. Once eggs have been laid, in May, and the maggots bore into the bases of bulbs, nothing will arrest the gradual yellowing of leaf tips, and the withering and rotting disintegration of attacked plants. Then the only measures left are, to pull up, thoroughly to crush and compost such plants (thus killing any maggots), so that the trouble is not perpetuated.

The only onion-fly repellent known to the writer is soot, which has been found useful, when repeatedly sprinkled or distributed in 1-inch bands along rows of susceptible plants during April and May.

POTATO BLIGHT (*Phytopthora infestans*)

Under moist and humid weather conditions in July and August (typical 'blighty weather'), the 'pores' of potato foliage open and can be invaded by the wind- or water-borne spores of the fungus, *Phytopthora infestans*. So far as the writer knows, this is true of both organically, and non-organically, grown potatoes; there is as yet no evidence to show that this physiological process of invasion is modified or prevented by raising potatoes on composted soil. There is, however, no dearth of reports from organic cultivators who claim immunity in bad areas and bad seasons. One of the many, by Professor W. Newcomb, is mentioned in *Organic Gardening* (U.S.A.), of June 1948. This grower records that in the fifth year of organic management of his garden, a yield of 292 lb. of clean potatoes was obtained from 14 lb. of new Scottish seed, *Arran Pilot* and *Epicure*. Three rows of these potatoes left uncomposted were *slightly* attacked by blight, but flavour and keeping-quality of the remainder of the crop were both good. Potatoes, grown in adjoining gardens on either side, in one case fertilized with Grow-more and in the other with ordinary 'artificials', produced negligible yields due to blight infestation. Although this, and similar, experiences indicate that the organic cultivator may be less at the mercy of the weather than is his orthodox counterpart, the beginner-composter should heed just as much the nation-wide alarm signals given by government departments, newspapers and broadcasting systems when the barometer warns of cloudy, muggy weather coincident with certain temperature readings.

For until conversion to organics is completed, he may well need bordeaux or burgundy mixture, the only control once blight has become established. He should need it less and less, however, for what he can do is to ensure for the crop the best possible growing conditions and, for the causative fungus, the least possible chances of survival. He will then see little blight, if any, and only so late in the season that it causes negligible damage, despite the fact that the air may be 'smelly with blight' in a bad area.

To apply maximum quantities of compost (15 tons per acre is not too much per year) and to use compost-grown seed and a good rotation, are obvious steps to take in the chancy game of raising a blight-free crop. Nitrogenous manures, especially those readily available inorganics, which may stimulate rank growth less resistant to pest and disease attack, should not be used, and the quick-acting limes should be shunned for they stimulate the nitrification process. It is inadvisable to plant potatoes in a very sheltered position (where moisture collects) or too close in the row, for thick foliage in which no air circulates contributes to bad factors of humidity and moisture. The job of earthing-up should be done thoroughly, and the soil be well-compacted, so that chances are reduced of the fungus being able to get straight to the tubers. No potatoes should be left in the soil at harvesting: they might over-winter the fungus.

Symptoms of infection are: black or brown lesions, and a grey, plum-like mould which appears on leaves which finally wither and die prematurely. An infestation started by a blighty tuber left in the soil from the previous year, usually shows in patches or discs or plants affected; if the fungus comes wind- or water-borne, the whole plot is usually peppered or blanketed with those affected. To spray against a bad infestation is the only successful control measure. *Before* harvesting (which should be done preferably in fine, dry weather), all diseased and clean haulm should be quickly and carefully cut at earthing-up level, collected, then composted with other available material. (Both the hyphae and spores of *Phytopthora infestans* are killed, in tubers as well as in tops, in a hot air current at 140° F. (60° C.).) No new leaves should be allowed to grow before the tubers are lifted, an operation which should be delayed for ten days to a fortnight after that of haulm-removal; this allows the topsoil to dry out somewhat, thus destroying some of the spores left on its surface. Care should be taken to get up every potato, for an infected tuber may over-winter (without rotting) and release the fungus during the

133

next season. The crop, having been dug, should be left lying on the surface of the soil for several hours, to dry out. Any tubers which bear characteristic dark, affected areas should be sorted and used immediately (not thrown into a ditch or left on the ground), and the remainder, when thoroughly dry, be clamped or stored. Even though a few infected tubers may be missed, go into the storage heap and shrivel or rot, they will not actively spread the disease or affect clean tubers. The cause of a clamp sinking is that a great many blight-infected tubers have heated up and half cooked the surrounding unaffected ones.

Where potato blight frequently occurs thoughtful gardeners have invariably grown only a First Early such as *Arran Pilot*. The haulm of First Earlies is usually dying when blight spores are active and the crop may be dug, dried and stored before blight damage to the tubers takes place. In recent years plant breeding stations in Ulster and Scotland have produced varieties (cultivars) which resist some races of blight fungi. *Maris Peer*, *Ulster Classic* and *Pentland Hawk* are examples. *Pentland Crown*, now widely grown in Britain, has no immunity to blight but rather oddly blight fungus seldom causes severe damage to crops of this cultivar.

SLUGS AND SNAILS

The dozen or so common species of slugs and snails possess all the advantages over the organic gardener. Each is hermaphrodite, omnivorous and mainly nocturnal, and is potentially capable (with a little help!) of starting a line of 2,000,000 progeny in a single year. Even an organically grown plant cannot be expected to withstand well-developed, strong mouthparts that can tackle even a plum stone, and slugs and snails scorn little as food.

To protect tender plants in a greenhouse, or in a seed frame, of which slugs and snails are the worst pests, there is considerable temptation to use poison baits. But to do so out in the open would be like trying to stop an army by putting in its way half a dozen elephant traps or, an even closer comparison, trying to deal with an epidemic of infectious diseases with the aid only of a bottle of smelling salts. Sheer numbers of these pests make the use of poisons somewhat ineffective; though it results in the death of some, and may produce a certain number of 'drunks', which recover, it leaves far more unaffected.

ORGANIC CONTROL OF PESTS AND DISEASES

Since even the orthodox cannot gain complete control, the organic gardener's attitude is, so far as is practicable, to make 'allies' of these scavengers of the garden (which come into the same category as vacuum cleaners, or crabs on a seashore), or to discourage or repel them. The former attitude is justified because it has been found, that to provide an easily available source of food in the form of decaying organic matter and small earthworms (the natural diet of slugs and snails) tends to keep attack from healthy, growing plants. Anyone who provides for slugs and snails an after-dark banquet of compost and wilted weeds, placed on the surface of the soil in the middle of a patch of brassica seedlings, can prove this. But the supply of chlorophyl-containing matter—which these pests must have to produce 'slime'—must be kept up, or slugs and snails will attack growing plants.

In the ordinary course of events, organic methods of cultivation (particularly 'no-digging') may have a similar discouraging effect on invasion as is effected by cultivation during a dry season of soils orthodoxly treated and low in organic matter. This measure is useful, up to a point, because the slimy underparts of slugs and snails are both sensitive and vulnerable to irritation and 'coking-up' (nuisances which can be caused by dust and dry soil), as also to abrasions (which can be caused by prickly organic matter). For these reasons, mulches or barrier deterrents are the control measures mainly used.

A very effective adhesive and irritant is fresh soot. It must be kept well away from tender plants, to which it is dangerous, by accurate placement, and not broadcast. If it is laid in a thin line round a precious row of transplants or, like a harbour wall, round a whole bed, no large-scale invasion is likely until a break in defences is caused by rain or high winds, or the soot loses its irritant quality. As it deteriorates quickly, it must be frequently renewed for this purpose. Freshly slaked powdered lime, wood ash, or coal ash which is extremely corrosive and alkaline, can be used in the same way. Wood ash and lime can safely be broadcast and, apart from their irritant effect, usefully help to reduce any tendency of the soil towards acidity, which favours these pests. Sharp river sand is very useful, if used as a surface dressing, especially round the crowns of plants, such as delphiniums. So, also is chaff, even human hair, weighted down here and there by small stones or clods.

The trapping of slugs and snails is a control method traditionally used in the small garden. These pests 'lay-up' under leaves, twigs and rubbish (one of the reasons for keeping a garden clean, particularly

ORGANIC CONTROL OF PESTS AND DISEASES

near houses and frames), until two or three hours after sunset, when they emerge to search for food. They are therefore most easily collected from their cool and moist sleeping-quarters during the daytime. Provide, for their bedroom furniture, flat pieces of wood placed on the surface of the soil, or half-skins of grapefruits and oranges distributed like igloos in various parts of the garden. These are easily seen and should be examined daily or as often as possible. Soup-plates filled with milk (which must be changed when it goes sour) will also catch many slugs, if sunk to brim-level and examined daily. Of the less pleasant outdoor occupations after dark, one is the hand-picking of slugs and snails by torchlight—by means of which over 60,000 of these pests have been caught and destroyed in one garden in a single year.

These control measures are not very effective against those small slugs, usually dark brown or black, which spend much of their time underground. Damage caused by them to potatoes and carrots can, however, be minimized by getting these, and other, roots up as early as possible. To leave them in the ground until October or November is asking for trouble. Cultural routine raking, hoeing and digging exposes many of these slugs to thrushes and blackbirds. The keen eye of the gardener may also see some slugs for crushing underfoot. Crushed slug is a welcomed delicacy to largish garden pool fishes. The burying of uncomposted wastes in the garden soil appears to lead to a build-up of the soil slug population. Apart from the songbirds and the carnivorous slug the gardener has other allies in his battle with slugs—toads, frogs, hedgehogs and slow-worms.

WIREWORMS

Although the click beetle has been observed, when trapped in a glasshouse, to attack the foliage of a cultivated crop, it normally feeds and breeds in grassland, hedgerows and waste patches. The damage is caused by the larvae of the beetle, wireworms, of which there may be one to three millions in an acre of topsoil—freshly cultivated grassland. These larvae vary in length from $\frac{1}{2}$ to $1\frac{1}{4}$ inches with age and species, and in colour from light brown to bright yellow. All are smooth and, not counting the head, have twelve 'squeeze-box' segments to their body, three pairs of legs to the first three segments and a pair of false feet (or 'suckers') to the last. It is during their four years (of slow growth) in the soil, before the larvae pupate and emerge as beetles, that havoc is wrought. Fortunately for the gardener, clean cultivation destroys good breeding conditions. The mature beetle prefers the paddock to the vegetable plot for laying eggs, and the ceaseless transformation from larvae to adult, and migration from cultivated land, gradually reduces numbers to the point where negligible damage is caused, even though several thousand wireworms to the acre remain, four or five years after land has been first broken. It is during this period of reduction that special control measures may be needed to protect vulnerable crops—indeed, most garden plants. Carnations, chrysanthemums, lettuces, potatoes and tomatoes are particularly prone to attack. Some varieties of peas and beans show some resistance, but about the only immune crop is flax.

Attack is usually worst during the first year after deturfing. The larvae, if deprived of their natural food of vegetable matter and the roots of grasses and weeds, turn to the seeds and the roots, the tubers and inside stems of cultivated crops. To extract as many larvae as possible from the soil, de-turf during the warmer months of the year, when wireworm activity is greatest in the top 2 or 3 inches of soil. (If turves obtained in this way are stacked, later they can with safety be used as loam, for they will rapidly be vacated by wireworms.) Choose, if possible, to do the job of de-turfing in the period between early March and late May, or in September or October, for the larvae retreat to the lower soil levels during cold weather and during hot periods (especially of drought).

The movement of wireworms from one level of the soil to another is important to the gardener, for one of his best control measures depends on it. The treatment to be adopted is, to top-dress wireworm-inhabited soil with about 1 cwt. of rape meal to the acre (roughly 3 oz. per square yard), in April or early autumn. Wireworms prefer this organic fertilizer even to decayed vegetation as food and, lured to the soil surface, enormous numbers are consumed by birds. This treatment can be repeated in autumn, if first tried in April and again in the second year but this is not often found necessary.

Insurance against attack of crop plants by wireworm is the provision of an alternative food supply. Compost and even sawdust mulches, which supply something like the wireworms' natural food have, in various experiments in which wireworm counts were taken, been found to attract vast numbers away from standing crops. Careful selection of the crop to follow a 'cleaning crop' on the reclaimed paddock or kitchen garden, can also help. Vulnerable crops should be shunned, if possible. Summer-planted brassicas sometimes miss the main activity of wireworms in spring and, by autumn, are often strong enough to withstand attack. Broad beans can survive fairly tough competition from weeds and are comparatively resistant to wireworm (some substance, toxic or repellent to this pest may, it is thought, be exuded by this crop's roots). Peas are somewhat less resistant, and nettle stings may make their harvesting a painful job. Beans, parsnips and spinach survive attack in most cases. The potato is a very vulnerable crop and although this vegetable is frequently advised as a 'cleaning crop' for growing in freshly taken over weedy gardens and allotments, the crop may be badly damaged by wireworms.

Wireworm activity in the soil can often be discouraged by rolling, and the back-gardener or owner of a small glasshouse can try various methods of trapping the larvae with 'lure crops' or baits. Cabbage, brussels sprout, or broccoli stems, split lengthwise and stuck obliquely to the ground, up to 6 inches in it, or to within 3 or 4 inches of the root (which then serves as a handle), at 2- or 3-foot intervals each way, need almost daily examination, as do faulty potatoes, or carrots, spiked on the end of a stick and buried 2 or 3 inches deep. The larvae, thus attracted, can be knocked into a bucket and destroyed or the 'traps' be crushed and composted. In heated glasshouse beds, seeds germinate quickly at high temperatures, and wireworms, if present, are usually very active near the surface of the soil. Wheat or oats, sown up to 3 inches deep, in drills roughly 3 feet apart, a month or less before the main crop is planted out, are usually attacked almost at once. After three weeks, when the cereals' shoots are well above ground, and inspection of part of the row reveals congregations of wireworms (anything from ten to twenty to the yard), the rows should be carefully lifted with a trowel and plants and pests be composted or destroyed. The trap crop is sometimes left to grow on, in which case it usually serves to divert attack from the crop proper.

SOME OBSERVATIONS ON ORGANIC
MANURES AND ACTIVATORS

A n activator accelerates the process of decomposition of the many different wastes in the compost heap. Usually animal manures are preferred as compost activators. True, a heap containing a high percentage of such lush green material as lawn mowings apparently requires no other activator. There is a feeling held by many organic gardeners that garden compost must be prepared with the aid of some animal residue. Sir Albert Howard mentions (in *An Agricultural Testament*, Oxford University Press) how attempts to make humus in Ceylon without animal wastes were not good. As has been stated earlier, it is better to use too little animal activator than too much. Although farmyard manure (where obtainable) may be used at the rate of a quarter by bulk of the total vegetable matter in a heap, this heavy rate is not necessary. Nowadays the back garden or allotment composter has to make a little animal manure go a very long way. Apart from farmyard manure, which is a mixture of litter and dung with the urine of mixed animals, the following manures are those more commonly used by the British gardener.

HORSE MANURE

Horse dung with or without urine-soaked straw or hay can be mixed with water to form a slurry. This makes for better activation than does wet or dry horse manure. A little horse manure, mixed in equal portions with cow or pig dung, gives these slow-heating, 'cold' manures a boost of the heating power they lack.

COW AND BULLOCK MANURES

Where these manures are used a more rapid activation will take place if horse dung or poultry droppings are mixed in. The familiar, crusty cow-pats of the farm road often remain unchanged for weeks in the small compost heap. Release of the nitrogen that still remains, also otherwise slow breakdown in the heap, can be speeded by soaking them for about forty-eight hours in water (just enough to cover them in a barrel or pail), then stirring the mixture and pouring the resultant slurry over the compost heap during its construction.

PIG MANURE

Pig dung can be used at the rate of one-eighth by bulk of the total vegetable wastes in the Indore heap. The heap should be built carefully and, if necessary, allowed a longer total composting period. The result will be as clean an end-product as from any other mixture. The 'coldness' of pig dung is often reflected in somewhat lower temperatures than usual for the first week or so of composting, especially in heaps built during the colder months of the year, but gradually heat is worked up to the point at which it effectively rules out any disease-risk. More rapid heating can be obtained by mixing horse or poultry manure, each nitrogen-rich and 'hot', with the slower-heating pig manure.

SHEEP, GOAT AND RABBIT MANURES

These manures are grouped together here because the gardener can never get as much of them as he would like. Sheep and goat droppings are best used wetted by turning them into a slurry by the addition of water. The backyard rabbit keeper usually finds the nitrogen-rich bedding already well-wetted with urine. These manures can be used at the rate of one-eighth by bulk of the total volume of mixed vegetable wastes in the Indore heap.

POULTRY AND PIGEON DROPPINGS

These have at least four times the plant food value as farmyard manure and they should be used rather sparingly in compost making. Both manures are often obtained in a sticky, messy condition and it is not easy to spread the stuff evenly in a layer over vegetable and household wastes. If they are dry they can be mixed with vegetable wastes before a heap is built. The whole mixture should then be wetted well before stacking. Droppings from commercial poultry establishments are rather suspect. It is feared that the droppings may contain many unpleasant residues from antibiotics, disinfectants and other chemical products. Pigeon fanciers are often at a loss as to how to rid themselves of fairly large quantities of pigeon manure, eggs and dead birds. You can find out names and addresses of local pigeon fanciers at your local railway station and very probably be regarded by a friendly pigeon fancier as a blessing from heaven. Always keep poultry and pigeon manure stored in polythene bags until you use it. It can stink if stacked in the garden and cause a nuisance to the neighbours.

OTHER MANURES

You can use manure from ferrets, guinea pigs, hamsters, parrots, canaries and budgerigars in compost making. Few organic gardeners care to use dog dung from kennels, though. Raw sewage should never be used and many gardeners are squeamish of emptying chamber pots on to the compost heap. Human urine, if you wish to use it, is best poured on to a heap of soil, peat or sawdust. The heap should be kept covered to prevent flies and smells. The urine-earth can be used to activate your compost heaps.

DRIED BLOOD

For some city dwellers this packeted animal activator may be necessary where there just are no animal wastes around. Use dried blood at the rate of a double handful to each large barrow-load of mixed vegetable wastes. When possible, the blood should be thoroughly mixed with all other heap ingredients; otherwise it can be sprinkled in its dry state on to layers of vegetable matter, lightly watered as the heap is built up, or first soaked for twenty-four hours, and added with the water which is to be used to moisten the heap at various stages during its construction.

FISH MANURE

This can also be bought and used in the same way as dried blood in the compost heap. Fish manures can smell 'fishy' and, if stored in the garden shed or used in a compost heap, they may attract rats and cats.

TREATED SEWAGE

Some local authorities used to supply sacks of treated sewage at a cheap rate to ratepayers. There may be some authorities which still do this. In the United States of America most cities and towns supply this organic manure free for collection at the plant site. Organic gardeners who follow the Bio-dynamic method have never favoured the use of sewage from sewage works. At the present time all organic gardeners are taking a new look at sewage. Sewage supplied by authorities in some rural areas may be just 'sewage'; sewage from many rural and all urban areas may not be 'sewage' as such but may contain large quantities of factory wastes including many heavy metals which can unbalance the garden soil. All keen organic gardeners are linked to one or more associations (see Appendix III) and these bodies publish or give advice about this and other current subjects.

PROPRIETARY ACTIVATORS

Organic gardeners who adhere to the Bio-dynamic method make use of special compost-making preparations originated by Dr. Rudolf Steiner. In all European Common Market countries there should be no real difficulty in buying Q.R. Compost Activator. This herbal preparation was evolved by the late Miss Maye E. Bruce. Use Q.R. as directed on the package. Organic gardeners do not use chemical activators. In many cases, publicity of their use seems to be little more than an attempt to sell chemicals, bought cheaply by the ton, in small packets for high prices.

APPENDIX II

SOME TERMS USED BY
ORGANIC GARDENERS

AEROBIC COMPOST

Garden compost made from varied wastes in the presence of air. Much of the decomposition of the wastes is carried out by bacteria needing a supply of air. Almost all garden compost is prepared aerobically.

ANAEROBIC COMPOST

Garden compost prepared in an airtight container. The wastes are decomposed by bacteria which exist without air. Some experiments have been carried out by this method which could be useful on a commercial scale where the waste products used include many very smelly items. Unless the gardener is careful anaerobic conditions can occur in the pit method of compost making. Anaerobic conditions can also occur in heaps if they are over-wet or too tightly packed. These conditions can lead to a malodorous mess rather than garden compost.

CHEMICALIZATION

This refers to chemicalization of the soil by those who consider that plants ought to be fed directly by chemical potions applied to the soil either before or during the growth of food crops. Organic gardeners consider this practice as dangerous to man and all life on this planet and to the soil itself.

COVER CROP

Sowing seeds of a quick growing subject in ground which is vacant for some months of the year. The cover crop protects the soil from hot sun, heavy rains and strong winds. Plant nutrients are not leached by rains but are taken up by the cover crop which is ploughed or dug into the soil. See also *Green Manuring*.

CROP RESIDUES

Many plant foods are present in those parts of a plant which man does not harvest for use. With peas, for example, man removes the seeds for use and leaves the pods, foliage and roots. If these wastes are burnt the ash is of negligible value. If the wastes are composted the plant foods are used by a crop grown in the ground to which the ripe compost is applied. The conservation of crop residues and their use in the compost heap is a typical organic gardening technique.

EROSION

A loss of top soil by its being blown away by winds or by its being washed away by heavy rain. Because of a lack of organic matter in many farm soils much erosion is taking place. The removal of hedges is a contributory factor in speeding up erosion. The false notions of soil chemicalization can lead to erosion. How dangerous erosion can be may be judged by what happened in the United States of America during the mid 1930s. The top soil was blown off entire counties leaving ground quite unsuitable for farming and gardening.

FERTILIZERS

Organic gardeners reject the use of all chemical fertilizers. Instead reliance is placed on garden compost to supply all plant nutrients with, where it is thought necessary, occasional feeds with liquid manure or liquid compost water. These feeds are prepared by soaking a small sack of animal manure or garden compost in a tub of water. The liquor is diluted so that it has the colour of very weak tea. Where a soil is not as highly fertile as it ought to be these feeds can help in the production of cucumbers, sweet corn, pumpkins, melons and vegetable marrows.

GARBAGE

Kitchen and household refuse contains much material for the compost heap. The use of these wastes in compost making helps to solve the problem of what to do with what really are valuable organic materials. Some local authorities make municipal composts. Household refuse forms a large part of the wastes used in the process. The resultant end-product is on sale but usually only to the large-scale user who buys the compost by the ton or by the truck load. Municipal composts, if made solely from urban waste products, may contain much ash from coal and smokeless fuels. Although most metal objects may be removed before the process starts, the compost may contain a proportion of metal. Although generally the organic movement is in favour of the composting of town wastes and violently opposed to their being burnt or dumped in the seas, some organic gardeners consider municipal composts may be more suited to land reclamation for park land rather than for use in soils where food crops are to be grown.

GREEN MANURING

Special crops, usually quick growers like mustard, are sown in vacant soil. These crops are known as 'green manures'. They may, when still young and succulent, be ploughed, forked or hoed into the ground or be added to the compost heap. There is little room in the modern, small garden for this practice. See also *Cover Crop*.

HUMUS

This is organic matter in a very advanced stage of decomposition. After garden compost has been applied to the soil the compost decomposes to humus. Humus not only contains plant foods but has a glue-like structure which prevents soil erosion.

MANURES

Usually this means animal manures. There are vast quantities of animal manures in Britain today. Most of them are the by-products of battery hens and livestock sweat boxes. These animal wastes are likely to be contaminated by chemical residues—hormones, vaccines, pesticides, disinfectants. The organic gardener using animal manure in small quantities in the compost heap likes to know the source of the manure and know that it is not chemically contaminated. Garden compost is a 'complete manure' because it contains all necessary plant foods.

MICRO-ORGANISMS

A vast number of bacteria, fungi and other minute creatures inhabit each square foot of healthy soil. Micro-organisms by the million exist in the compost heap. Most micro-organisms are necessary for the good health of the soil and for good health in plants.

APPENDIX II

Some factory-made chemicals are likely to kill or reduce the number of micro-organisms.

MULCH

This is a soil cover laid down around garden subjects to conserve moisture, prevent weeds or (in winter) to maintain a higher soil temperature. Most mulches are organic. Examples are lawn mowings, autumn leaves, straw, sawdust and wood shavings. All gradually rot down and enrich the soil. Garden compost is an excellent mulch but there is seldom sufficient compost around for its use as a mulch.

NO-DIGGING

A method of gardening (usually all-organic) in which little or no soil disturbance is practised. Instead, the soil surface is mulched heavily with garden compost and with either peat or sawdust. The method is sometimes confused with *Organic Surface Cultivation* (see below).

ORGANIC MATERIALS

These are animal or vegetable wastes which are used in organic gardening to promote the well-being of the soil. Most wastes reach the soil after fermentation and partial decomposition in the compost heap.

ORGANIC SURFACE CULTIVATION

A term often used as a synonym for *No-Digging*. But almost all organic gardeners reject all deep digging and soil inversion. The organic gardener increases the fertility and improves and conserves the structure of the top soil. Thus the spade is more likely to be used as a planting tool rather than for digging in the organic garden. Organic surface cultivation involves the use of mulches, too.

TRACE ELEMENTS

Plant nutrients needed in minute quantities by growing plants. Without the correct quantities of trace elements plants are weak and the weakness is passed on to the consumer—man and his domestic animals. An excessive quantity of trace elements can lead to a sick soil and to sick plants. Most soils in Britain originally had a sufficient supply of trace elements at the correct rate for optimum plant growth. Deficiencies have taken place due to intensive cropping, erosion and chemicalization of the soil. Trace elements can be replaced by the chemist but at possibly wrong proportions. The adding of trace elements to mixtures of chemical fertilizers is a potential hazard to the well-being of the soil. Where garden compost is prepared from many varied wastes originating from many different sources there are trace elements present but never in excess. The organic gardener likes to incorporate wastes from all parts of Britain and throughout the world in his or her compost heaps and it is in the home itself that vast quantities of varied wastes from here, there and everywhere are found for composting.

SOME ORGANIZATIONS CONCERNED WITH THE ORGANIC METHOD OF GARDENING

The Bio-Dynamic Agricultural Association, Broome Farm, Clent, Stourbridge, Worcestershire.

The Canadian Soil Association of Organic Husbandry, 166 Joicey Boulevard, Toronto 12, Ontario, Canada.

The Henry Doubleday Research Association, 20 Convent Lane, Bocking, Braintree, Essex.

The Organic Gardening Association of Southern Africa, P.O. Box 47100 Parklands, Johannesburg, South Africa.

The Organic Gardening and Farming Club, 4373 Paret Road, Kelowna, British Columbia, Canada.

The Organic Gardening and Farming Society, Box 2605W, Melbourne 3001, Australia.

Organic Gardening and Farming Society of Tasmania, 12 Delta Avenue 7006, Hobart.

The Soil and Health Foundation, 33 East Minor Street, Emmaus, Pennsylvania 18049, U.S.A.

Soil Association Ltd., Walnut Tree Manor, Haughley, Suffolk.

The Soil Association of New Zealand, 22 Collins Street, Addington, Christchurch, New Zealand.

The Soil Association Group of South Australia, 9 Cotham Avenue, Kensington Park, S. Australia 5068.

PERIODICALS

The Journal of the Soil Association—New Bells Press, Walnut Tree Manor, Haughley, Suffolk, England.

Organic Gardening and Farming, 33 East Minor Street, Emmaus, Pennsylvania 18049, U.S.A.

INDEX

INDEX

INDEX

Salt (common), 126
Sandy soil, 111, 112
Sawdust, 16, 35, 64, 73, 74, 76, 77, 95, 100
Scott, J. C., 90
Seaweed, 77 ff., 96, 106, 111
Septic tank, 54, 91, 93
Sewage (and sewage sludge), 90, 91, 141
Slugs, 35, 37, 122, 134 ff.
Snails, 134 ff.
Soap (soft), 123
Soil Association Ltd., The, 90
Soil blocks, 98
Soil conditioners, 113, 114
Soot, 132, 135
Spent hops, 63, 66
Steiner, Rudolf, 124, 142
Stem eelworm, 87
Straw, 16, 48, 53, 56, 63, 64, 81 ff., 95, 96, 108
Straw bales, 32, 47
Strawberry Mite, 87
Subsoiling, 111, 113
Sulphate of ammonia, 21, 54, 105, 122
Sulphate of potash, 99
Sulphur, 18, 20
Surface cultivation, 110 (*see also* No-digging)

Surface cultivator, 42

Tea leaves, 68
Thermophils, 26
Toads, 121
Trace elements, 18, 19, 54, 106, 112, 146
Turf, 29, 97

Urine, 38, 141

Vegetable material (for compost-making), 36
Viruses, 89, 90
Vuren, J. P. J. van, 90

Wasps (hymenopterous), 124
Water weed, 84 ff.
Watson, E. F., 89
Weeds (for compost-making), 36, 96
Weeds (host plants), 123, 127, 131
Windbreak, 29
Wireworms, 136 ff.
Wood shavings, 64, 73, 74, 77

Yew leaves, 70

Zinc, 18